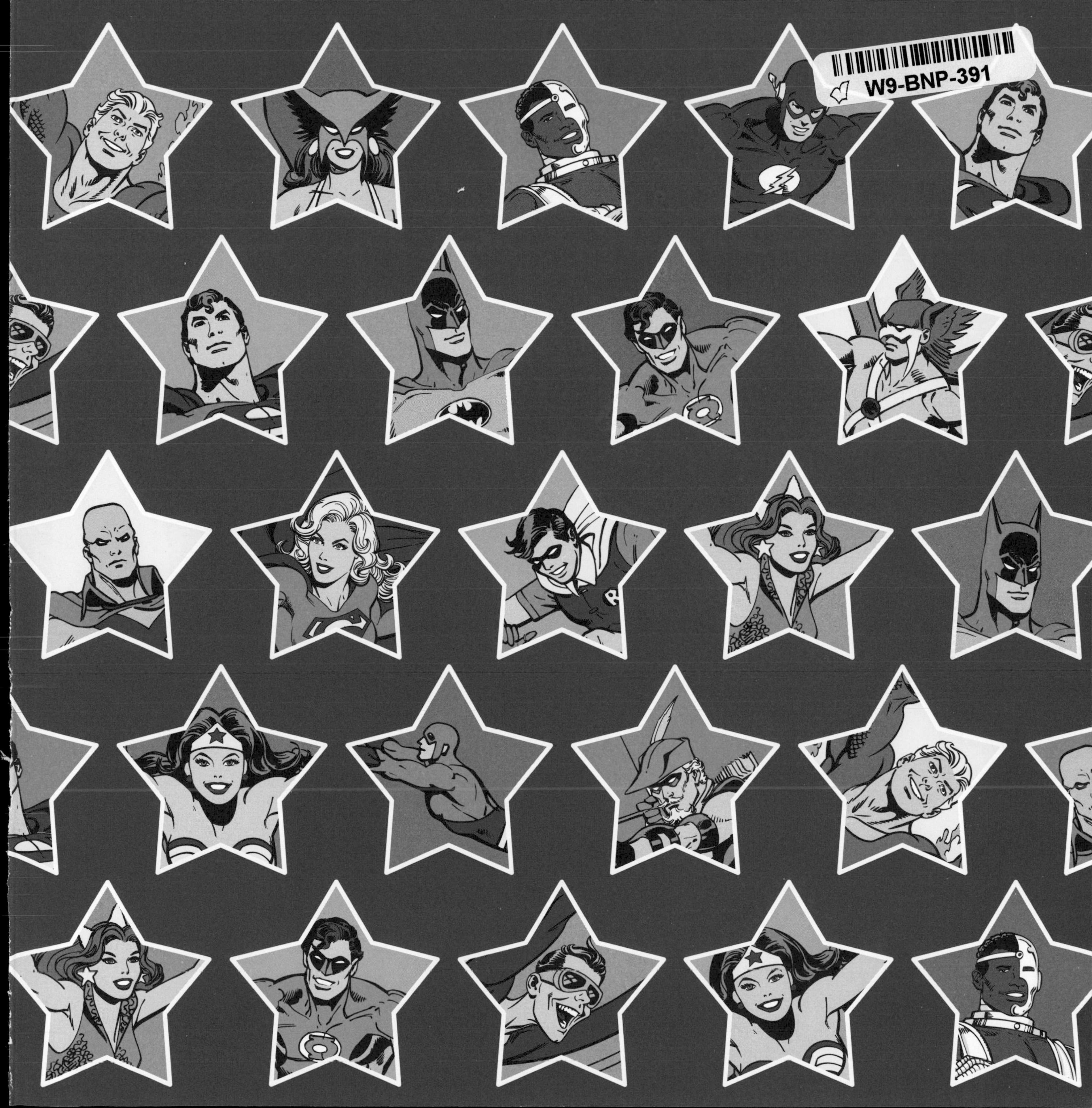

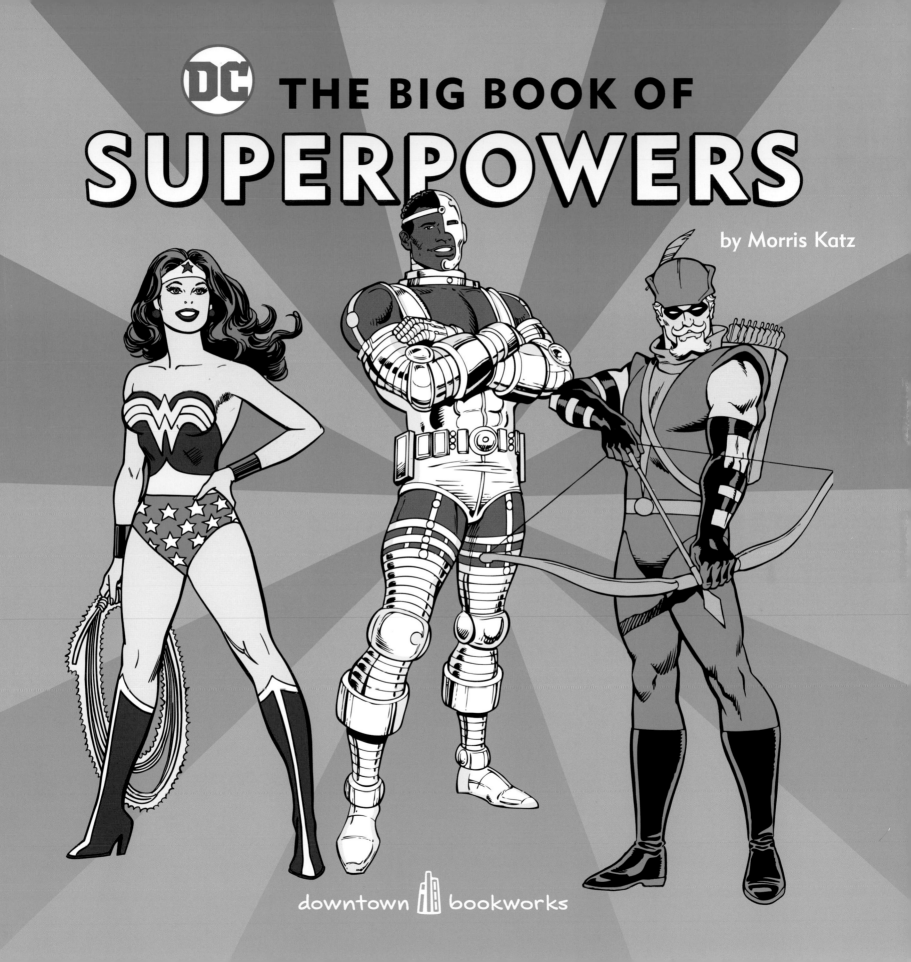

THE BIG BOOK OF
SUPERPOWERS

by Morris Katz

downtown bookworks

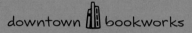 downtown bookworks

Downtown Bookworks Inc.
265 Canal Street
New York, New York 10013
www.downtownbookworks.com

Designed by Georgia Rucker
Typeset in Geometric and HouseSlant
Printed in China
June 2016
ISBN 978-1-941367-24-7
10 9 8 7 6 5 4 3 2 1

Thanks to Aaron for the big idea!

INTRODUCTION

Some super heroes came to Earth with alien powers. Others got their abilities as the result of freaky accidents. And some worked really, really hard to master their skills, such as martial arts. Discover the amazing and inspiring stories of DC's super heroes and heroines!

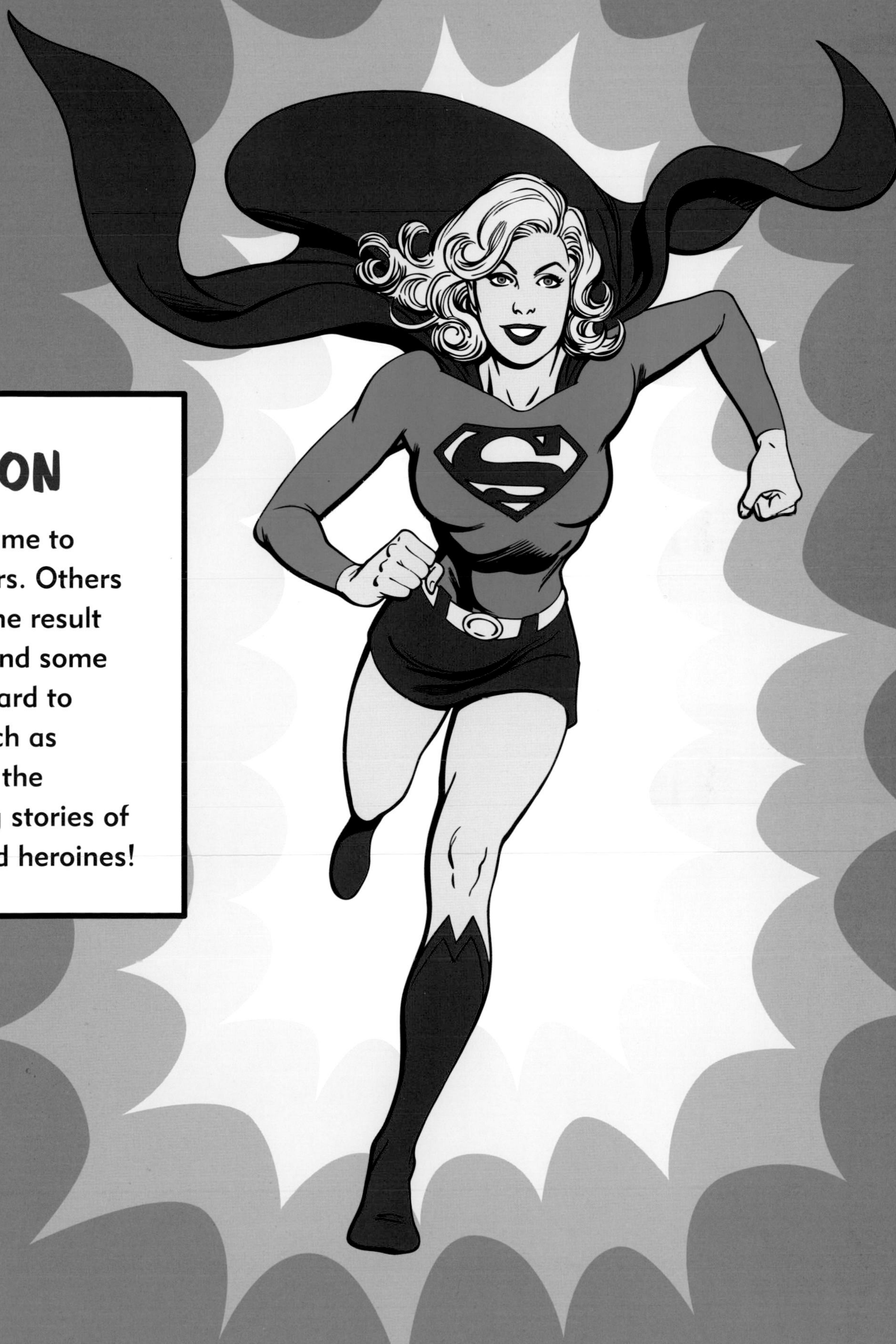

SUPERMAN™

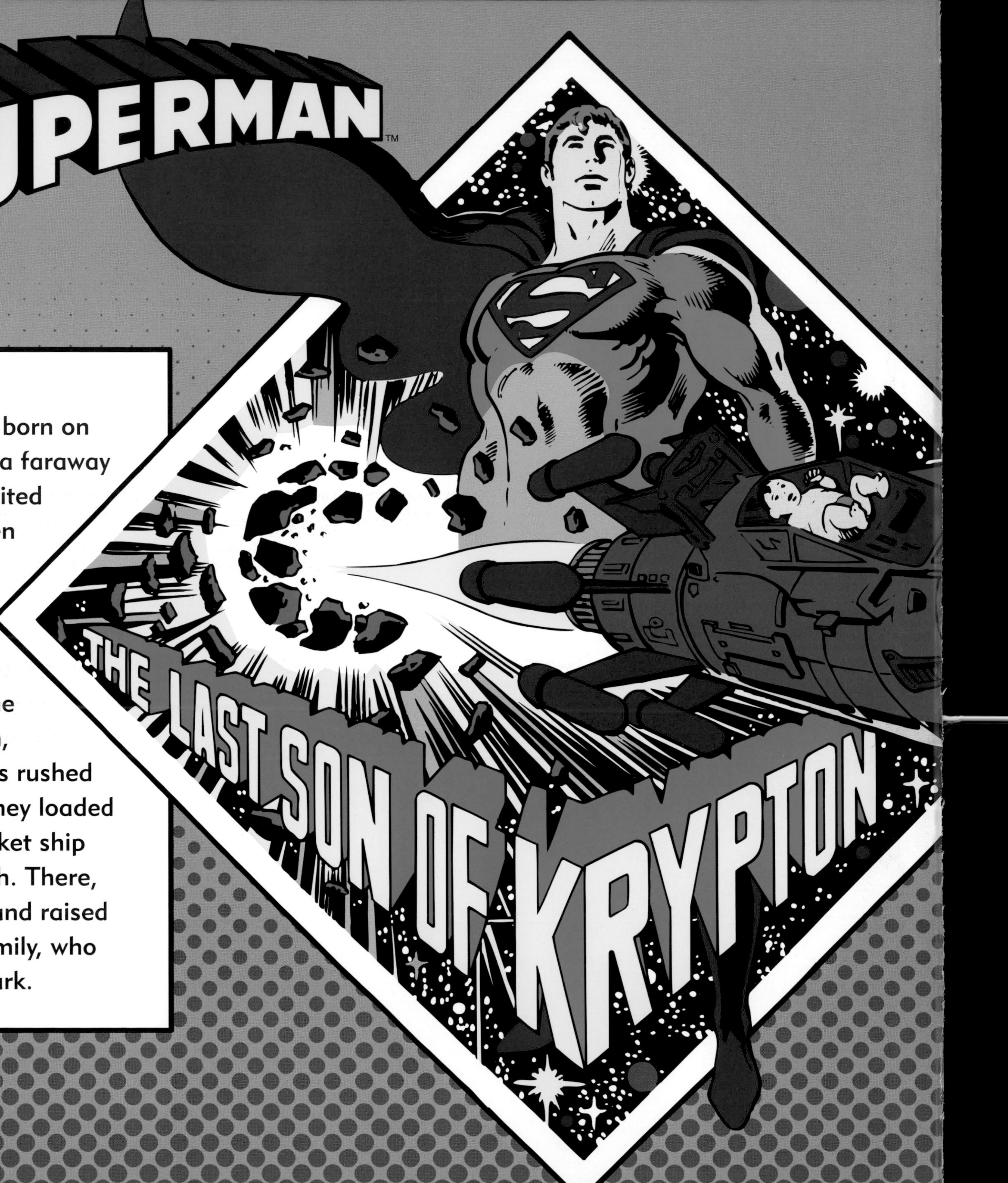
THE LAST SON OF KRYPTON

Kal-El was born on Krypton, a faraway planet that orbited a red sun. When he was a baby, the planet's radioactive core exploded. Right before the giant explosion, Kal-El's parents rushed to save him. They loaded him onto a rocket ship bound for Earth. There, he was found and raised by the Kent family, who named him Clark.

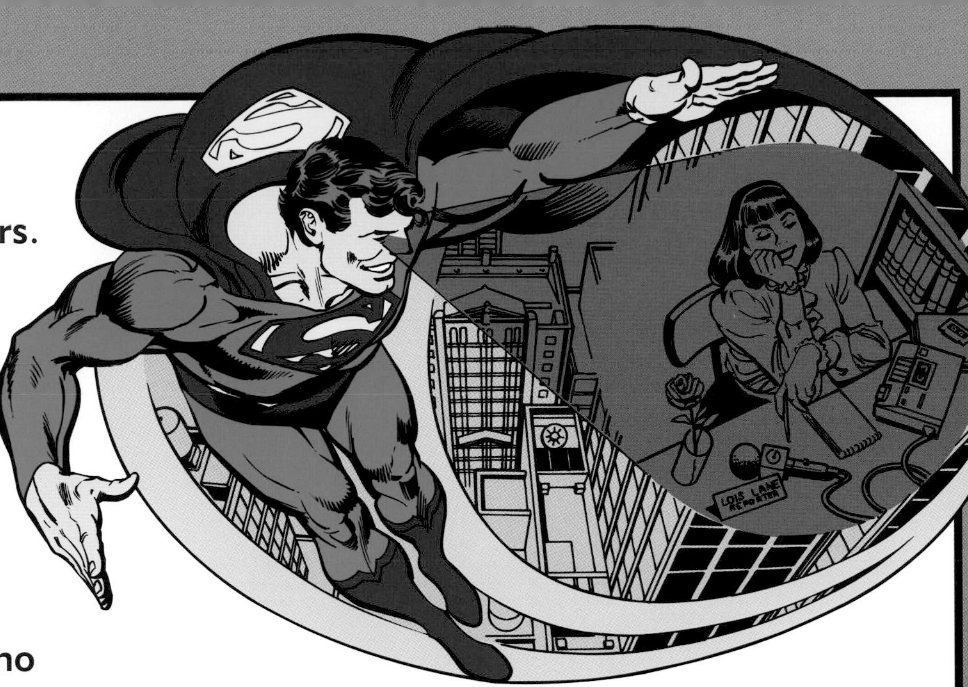
LOIS LANE REPORTER

As Clark grew older, he discovered his many superpowers. The yellow sun gave him super-strength, super-speed, X-ray vision (the ability to see through solid objects, like walls), and heat vision (the power to burn or melt objects, such as cars, just by looking at them). Clark could also fly. It's no wonder people began to call him Superman.

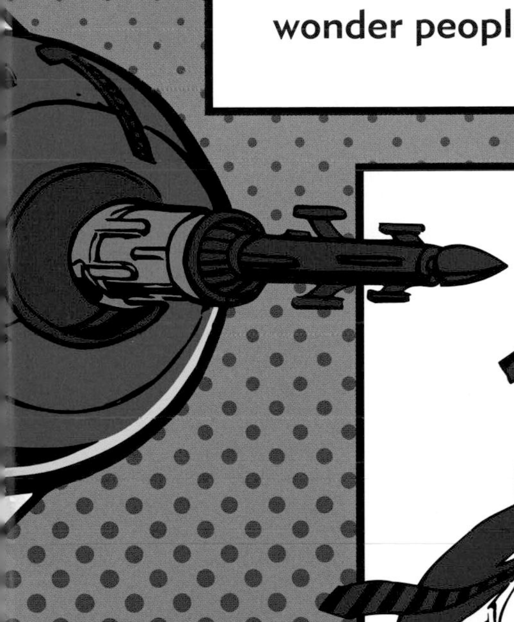

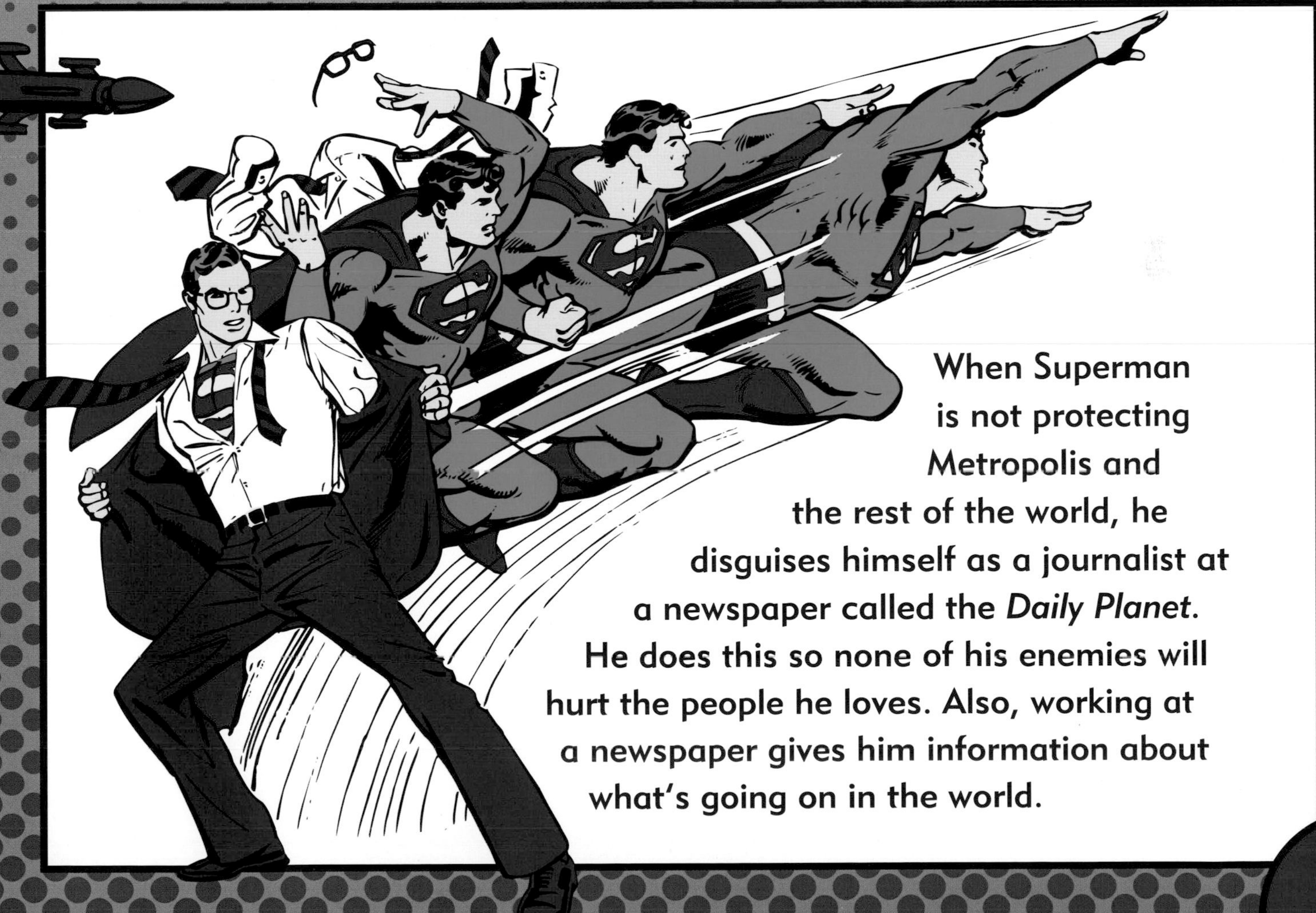

When Superman is not protecting Metropolis and the rest of the world, he disguises himself as a journalist at a newspaper called the *Daily Planet*. He does this so none of his enemies will hurt the people he loves. Also, working at a newspaper gives him information about what's going on in the world.

Supergirl is Superman's cousin. She comes from Krypton, too. Supergirl and Superman have the same incredible powers, but their pets, Streaky and Krypto, don't always get along.

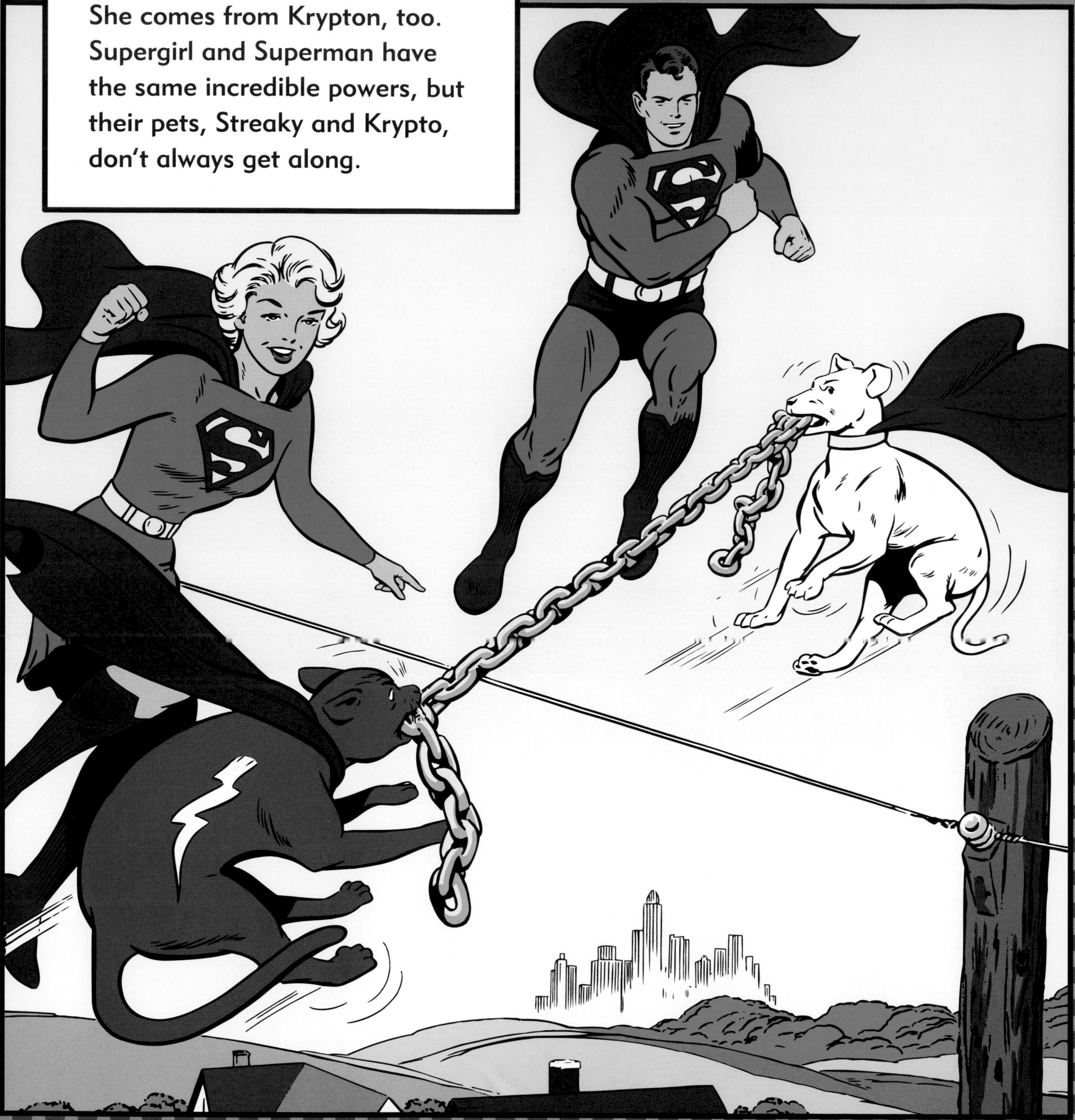

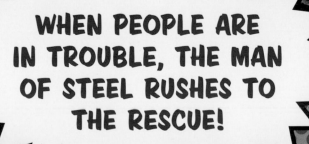

WHEN PEOPLE ARE IN TROUBLE, THE MAN OF STEEL RUSHES TO THE RESCUE!

BATMAN™

Bruce Wayne was born into a very wealthy family in Gotham City. When he was a child, his parents were killed by a robber. His butler, Alfred, took care of him. But Bruce never forgot his parents and did not want anyone to suffer like he had, at the hands of a criminal.

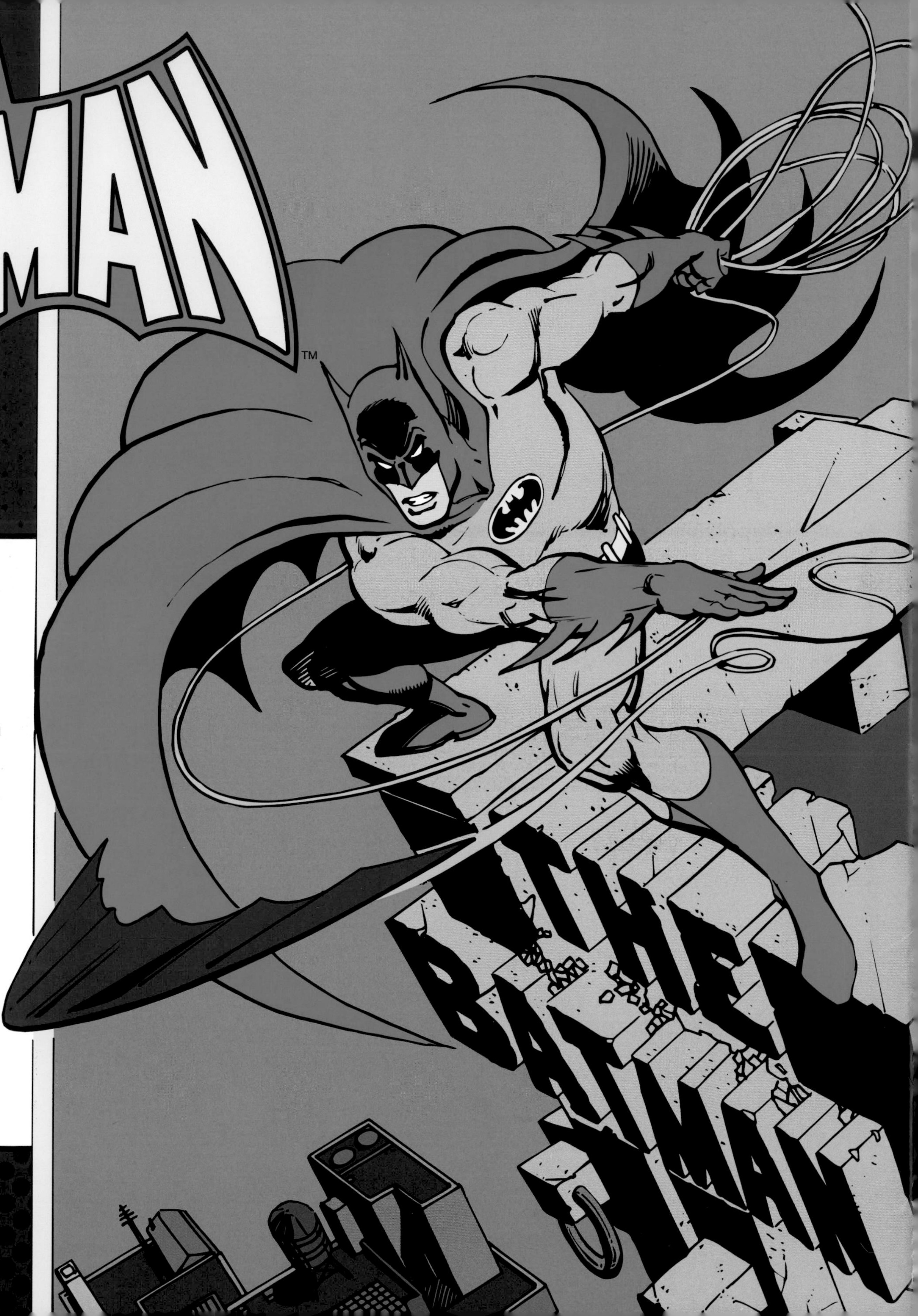
THE BATMAN

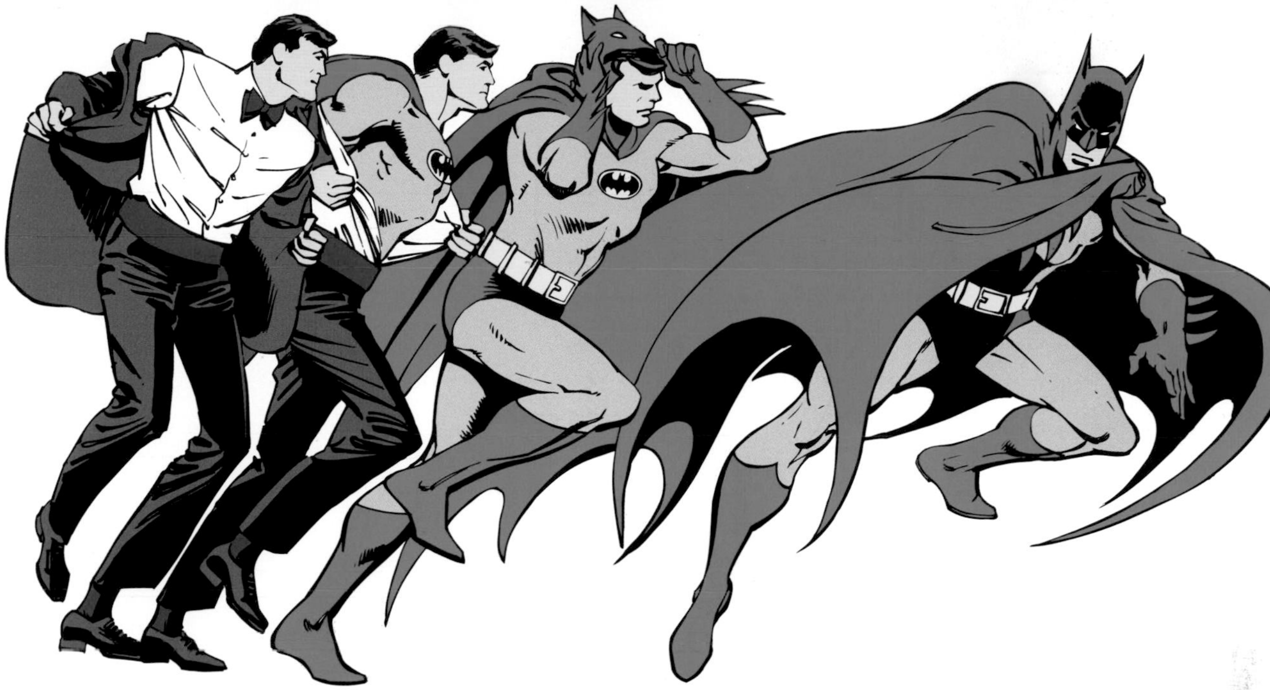

As he grew up, he trained in hand-to-hand combat and martial arts. Martial arts are different forms of fighting or self-defense, such as karate or judo. He exercised to build his muscles, and he practiced his fighting skills all the time. He took on the name Batman and built a secret hiding place, the Batcave. In it, he invented amazing tools to protect himself and the people of Gotham City. He built a Batmobile—a special car that can float or fly. And he designed a Utility Belt with all of the gadgets he would need to fight super-villains, like a Batrope and a Batarang. His Batcomputer helps him locate villains and know when and where he is needed.

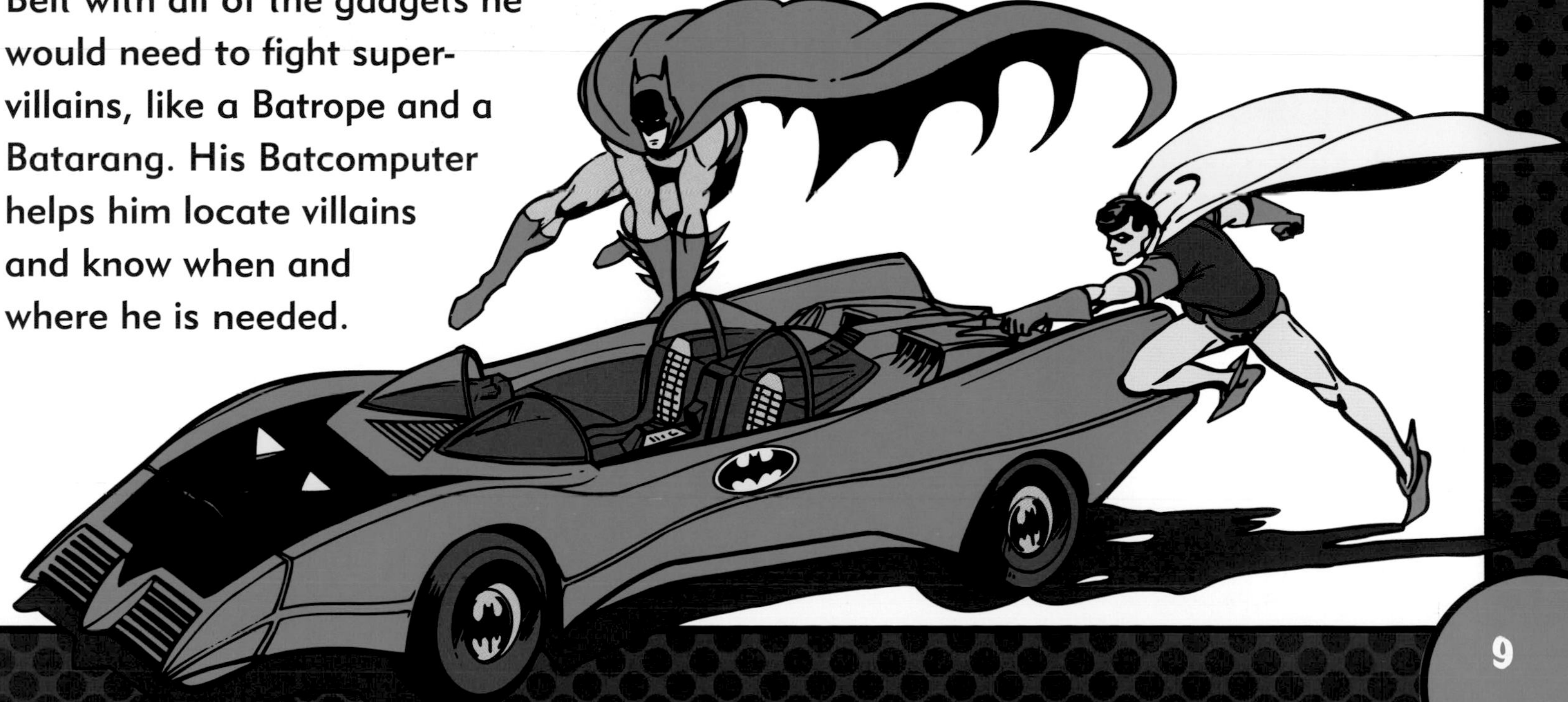

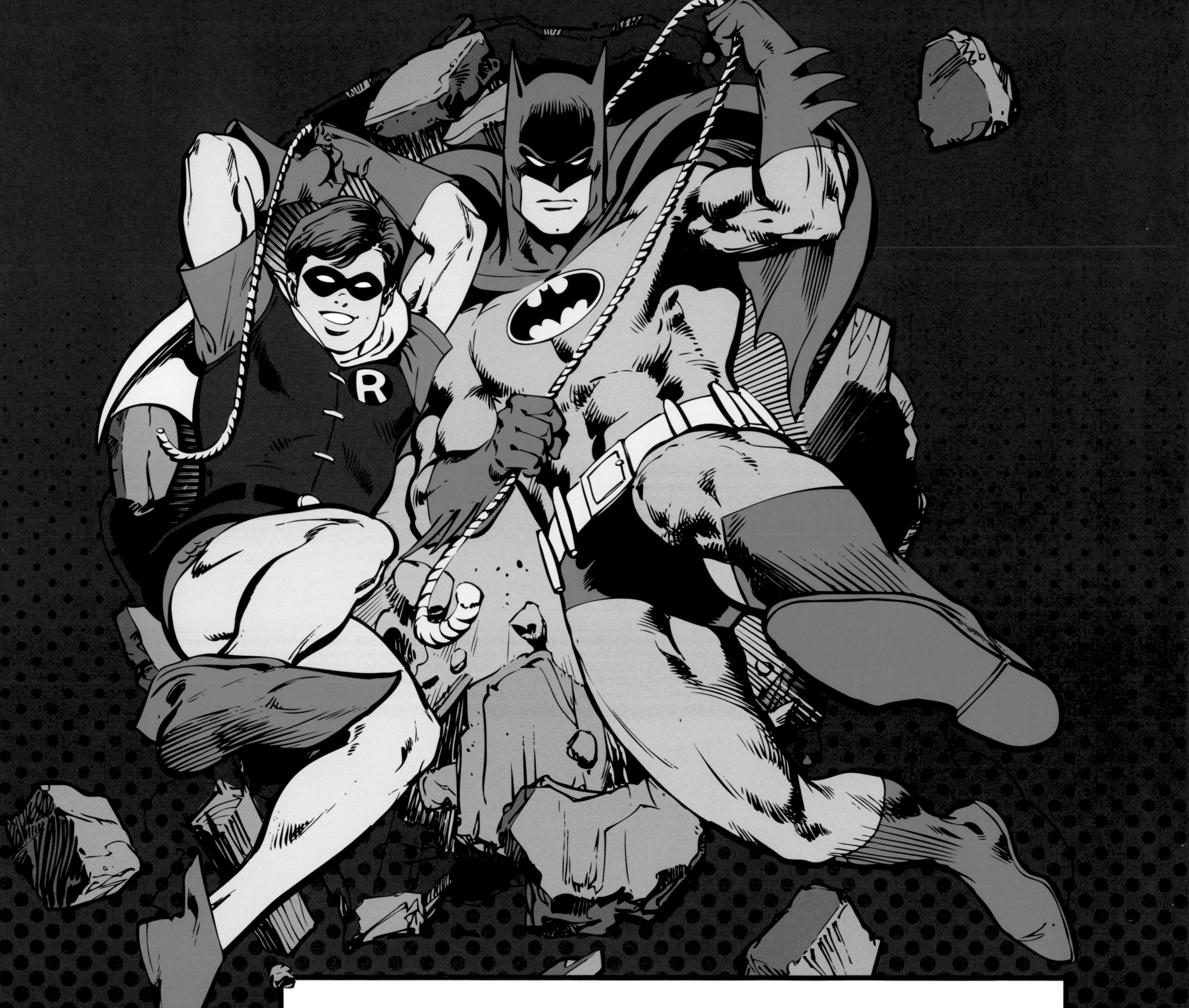

Batman met Dick Grayson when Dick was a trapeze artist in the circus. Dick had also lost his parents. Batman began to train him, and he became Batman's sidekick, Robin.

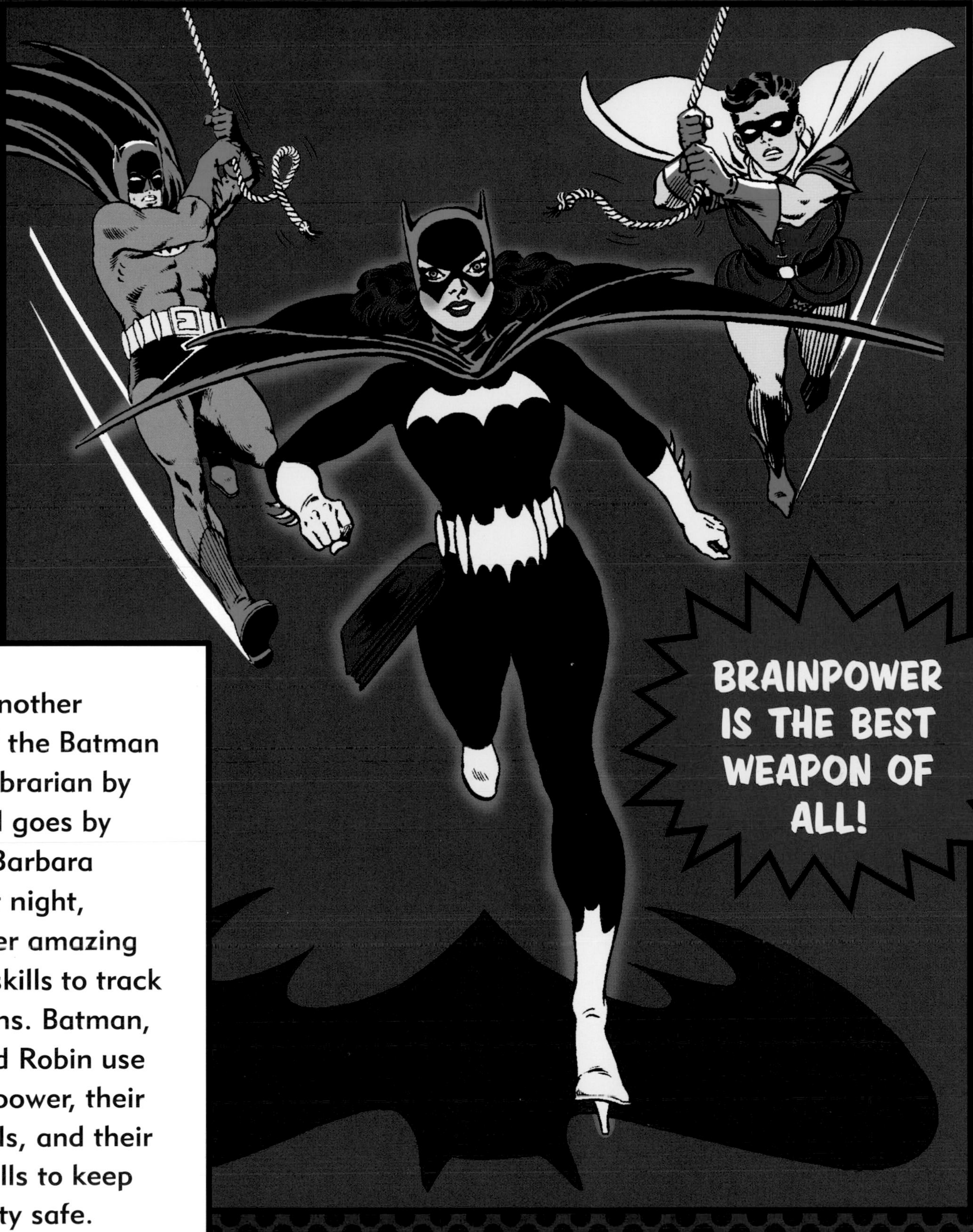
BRAINPOWER IS THE BEST WEAPON OF ALL!

Batgirl is another member of the Batman Family. A librarian by day, Batgirl goes by the name Barbara Gordon. At night, she uses her amazing computer skills to track down villains. Batman, Batgirl, and Robin use their brainpower, their special tools, and their fighting skills to keep Gotham City safe.

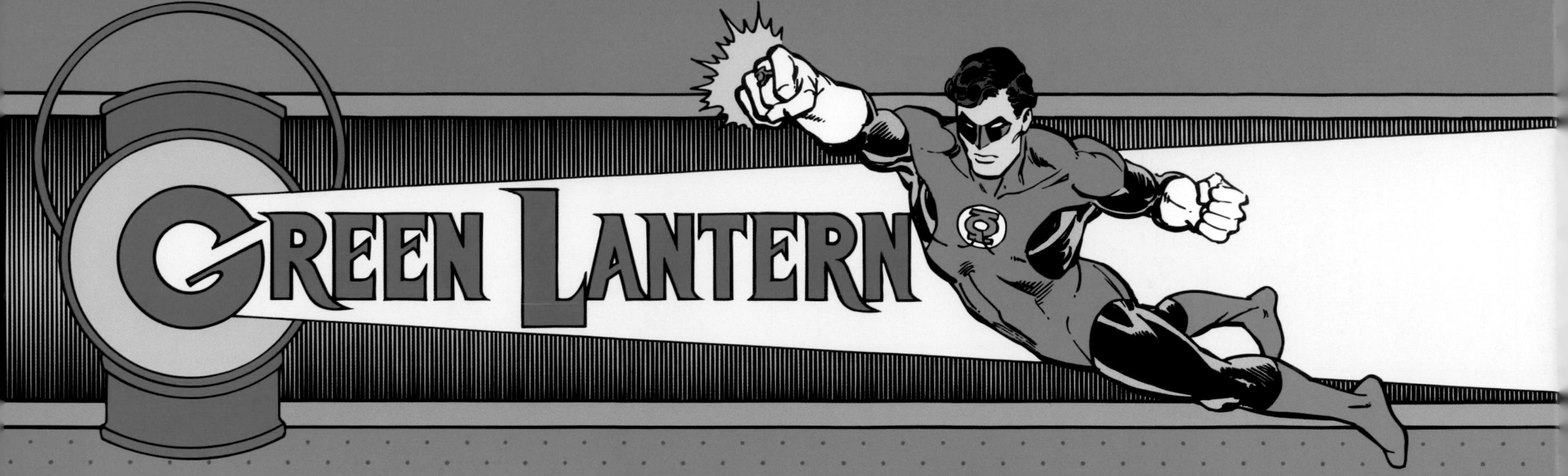
GREEN LANTERN

Green Lantern's power ring harnesses the forces of the universe. The ring itself decides who is brave and honest enough to wear it. When Green Lantern wears the ring, he can generate force fields, fire energy blasts, fly at supersonic speeds, and create solid objects made of pure energy. So it's really important to keep that ring charged!

When it's time to recharge his ring on the Power Battery, he recites the Green Lantern oath:

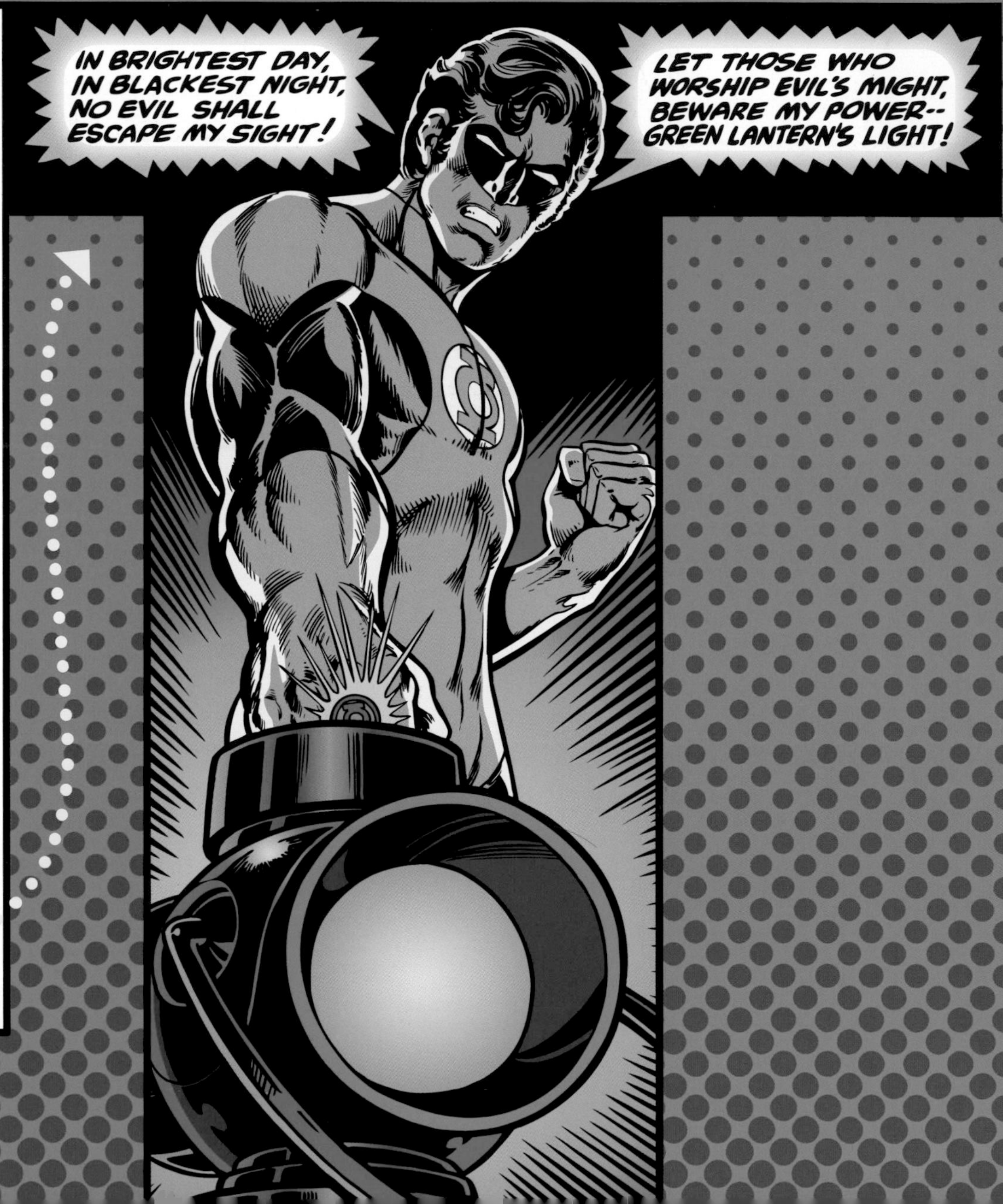
IN BRIGHTEST DAY, IN BLACKEST NIGHT, NO EVIL SHALL ESCAPE MY SIGHT!
LET THOSE WHO WORSHIP EVIL'S MIGHT, BEWARE MY POWER-- GREEN LANTERN'S LIGHT!

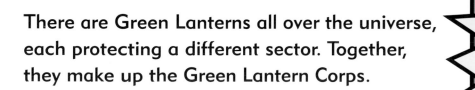

There are Green Lanterns all over the universe, each protecting a different sector. Together, they make up the Green Lantern Corps.

GREEN LANTERNS MUST BE BRAVE AND KIND TO EARN THEIR POWERS.

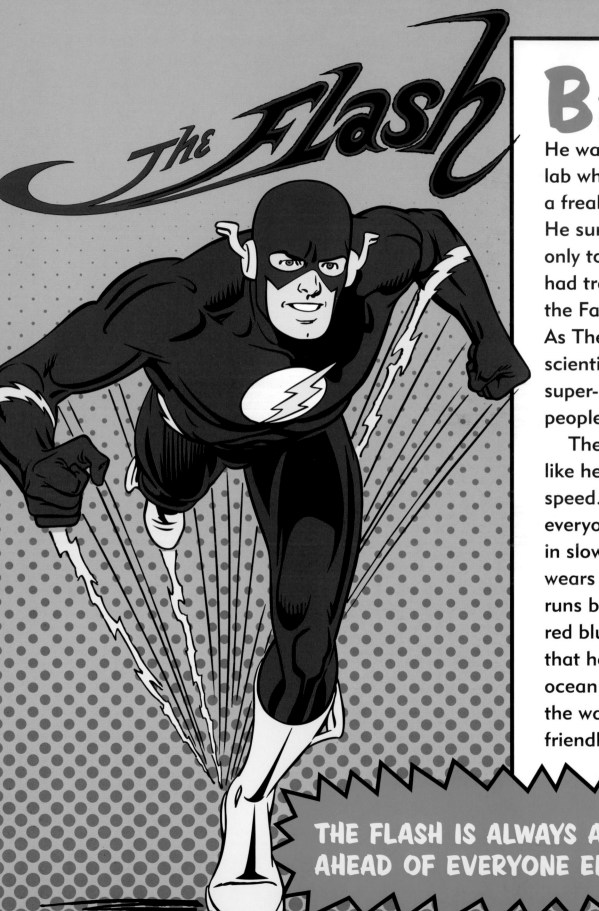

The Flash

Barry Allen was a brilliant scientist. He was hard at work in his lab when he was struck by a freak bolt of lightning. He survived the accident only to discover that it had transformed him into the Fastest Man Alive! As The Flash, he uses his scientific brain and his super-speed to protect the people of Central City.

The Flash does not feel like he's moving at super-speed. To him, it looks like everyone else is moving in slow motion. The Flash wears all red, and when he runs by, people see only a red blur. He moves so fast that he can run across the ocean without sinking into the water. He's one of the friendliest super heroes.

THE FLASH IS ALWAYS AT LEAST ONE STEP AHEAD OF EVERYONE ELSE IN THE WORLD!

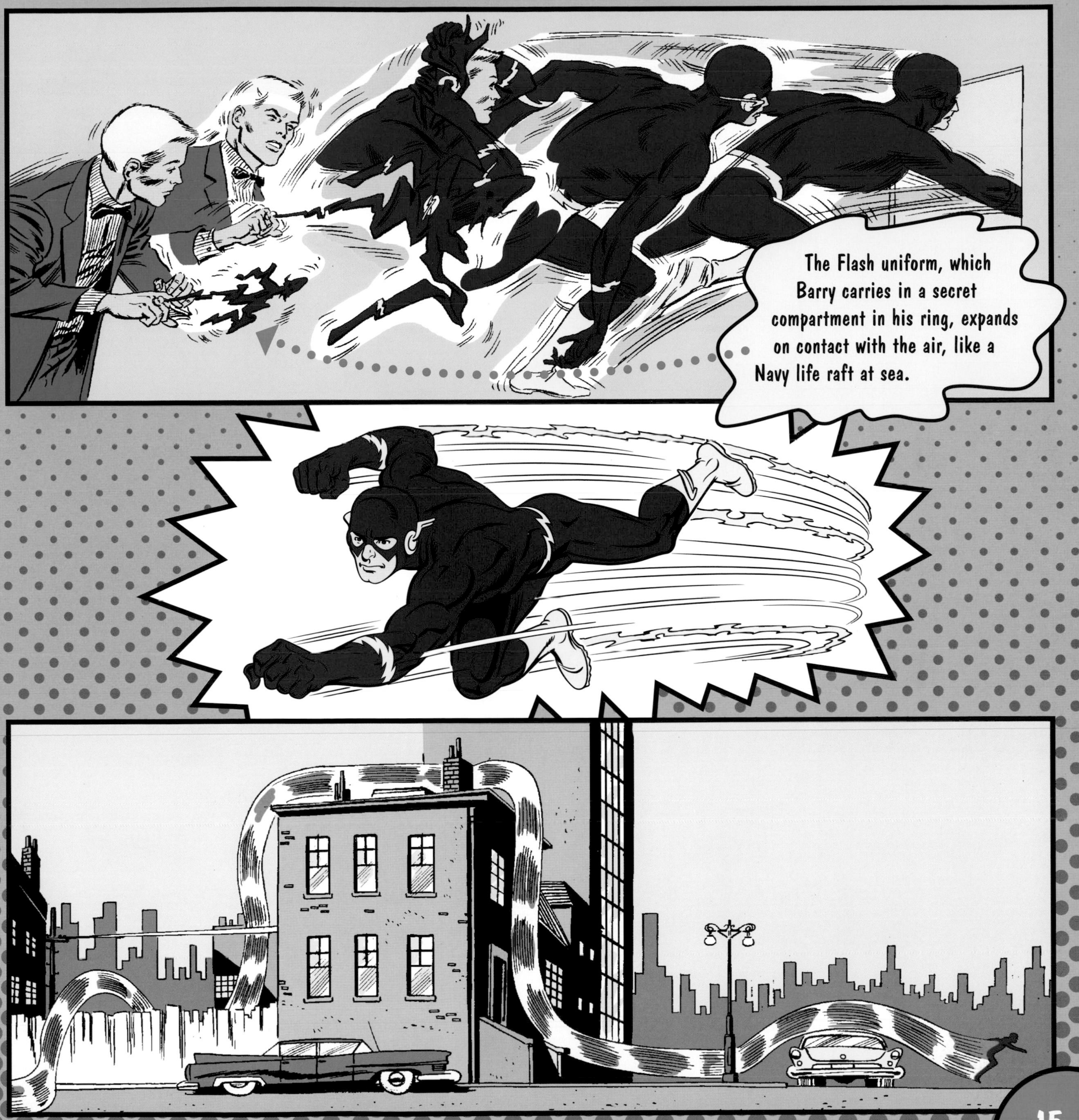
The Flash uniform, which Barry carries in a secret compartment in his ring, expands on contact with the air, like a Navy life raft at sea.

WONDER WOMAN

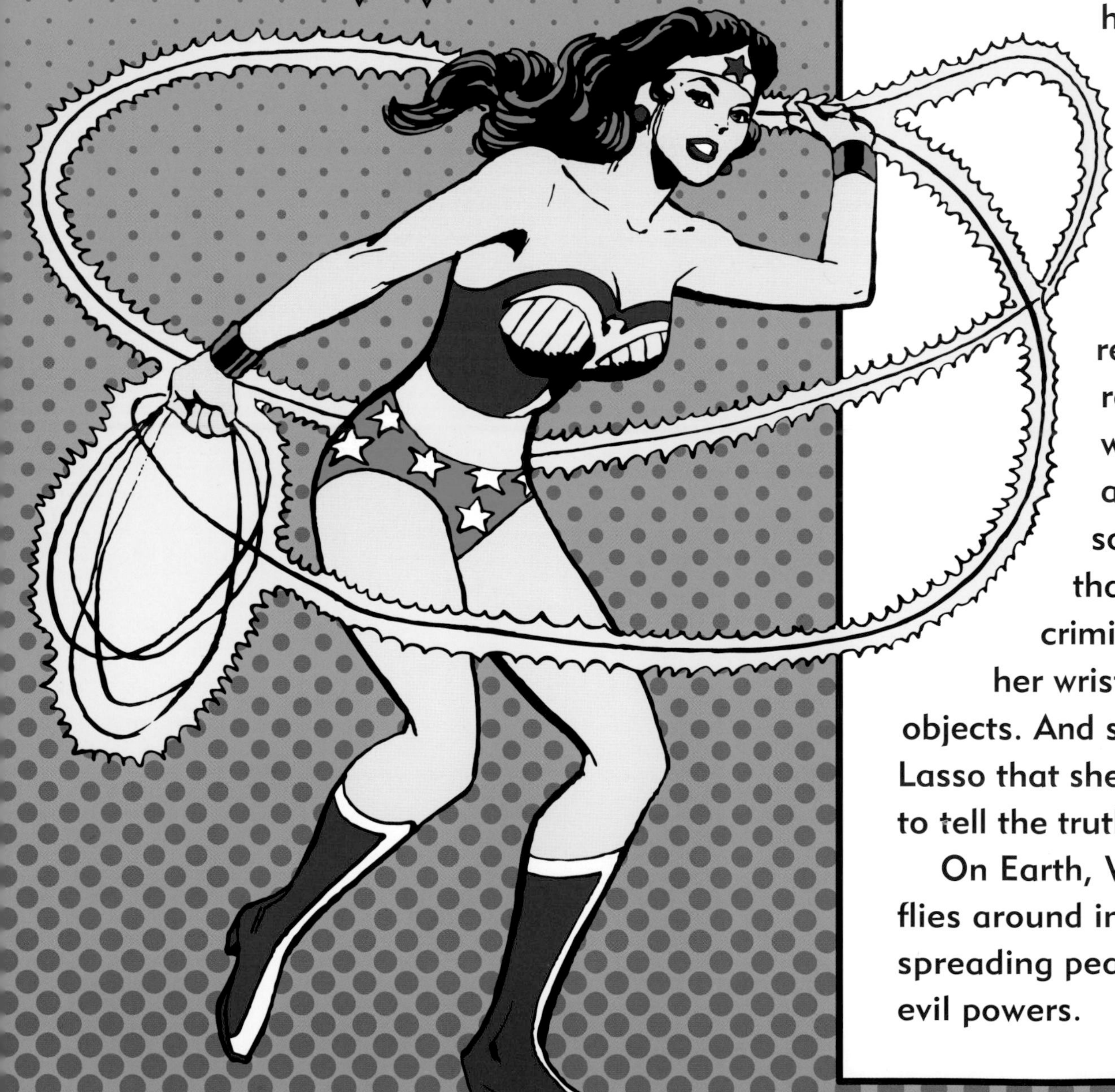

Wonder Woman started out as Diana, a princess. Her homeland was a peaceful island, filled with other Amazons—super-strong women like her. When Diana heard about other places where there were villains and fighting, she decided to leave her home to help people in need.

Wonder Woman is one of the strongest people on Earth! With her superhuman reflexes, she can react faster than the world's most talented athletes. She also has some special tools that help her defeat criminals. The cuffs on her wrists deflect dangerous objects. And she has a Golden Lasso that she uses to force people to tell the truth.

On Earth, Wonder Woman flies around in her Invisible Jet, spreading peace and fighting evil powers.

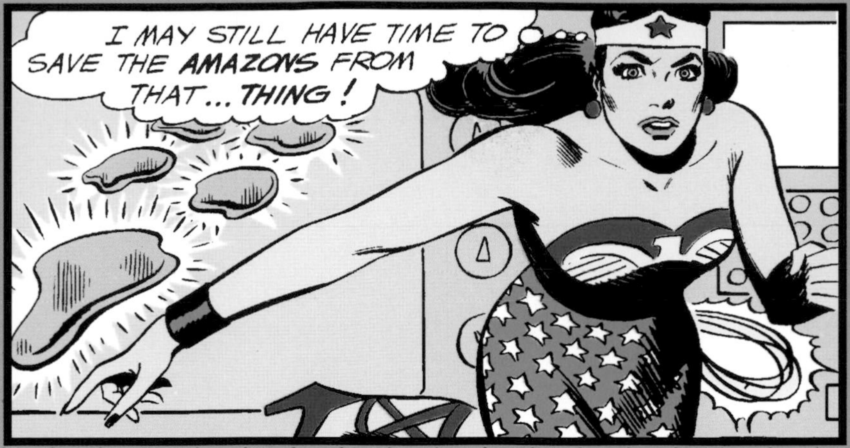
I MAY STILL HAVE TIME TO SAVE THE AMAZONS FROM THAT... THING!

FOR WONDER WOMAN, HELPING OTHERS IS EMPOWERING.

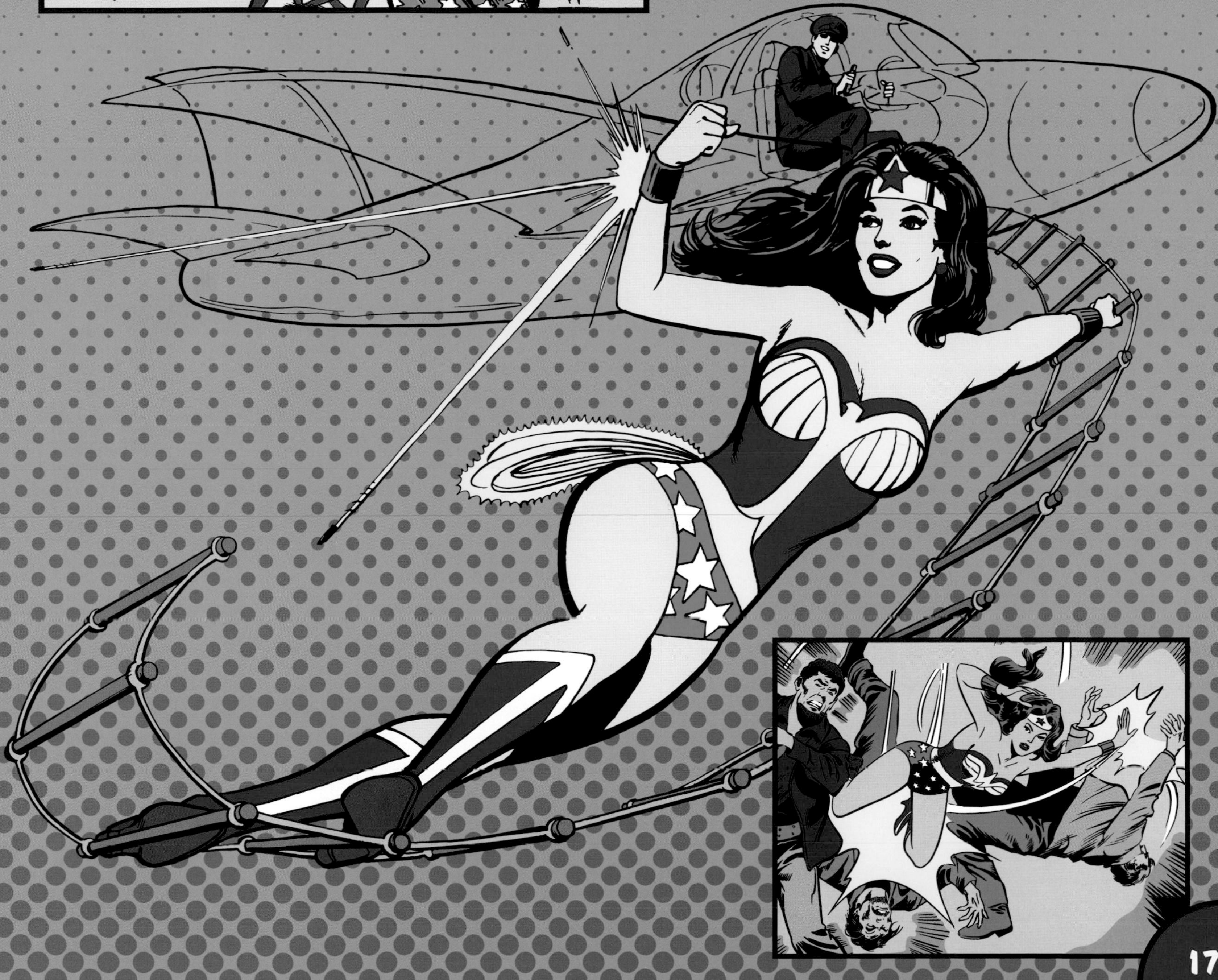

The Winged Wonders

Hawkman and Hawkgirl come from the planet Thanagar. They fly through the air with the help of enormous, feather-covered wings. They wear a special metal from Thanagar, called Nth Metal, which gives them healing powers. Like others from their home planet, they have super-strength.

Hawkman and Hawkgirl care a lot about the environment. Protecting the Earth's oceans and forests and air is a huge job. Luckily, they work together.

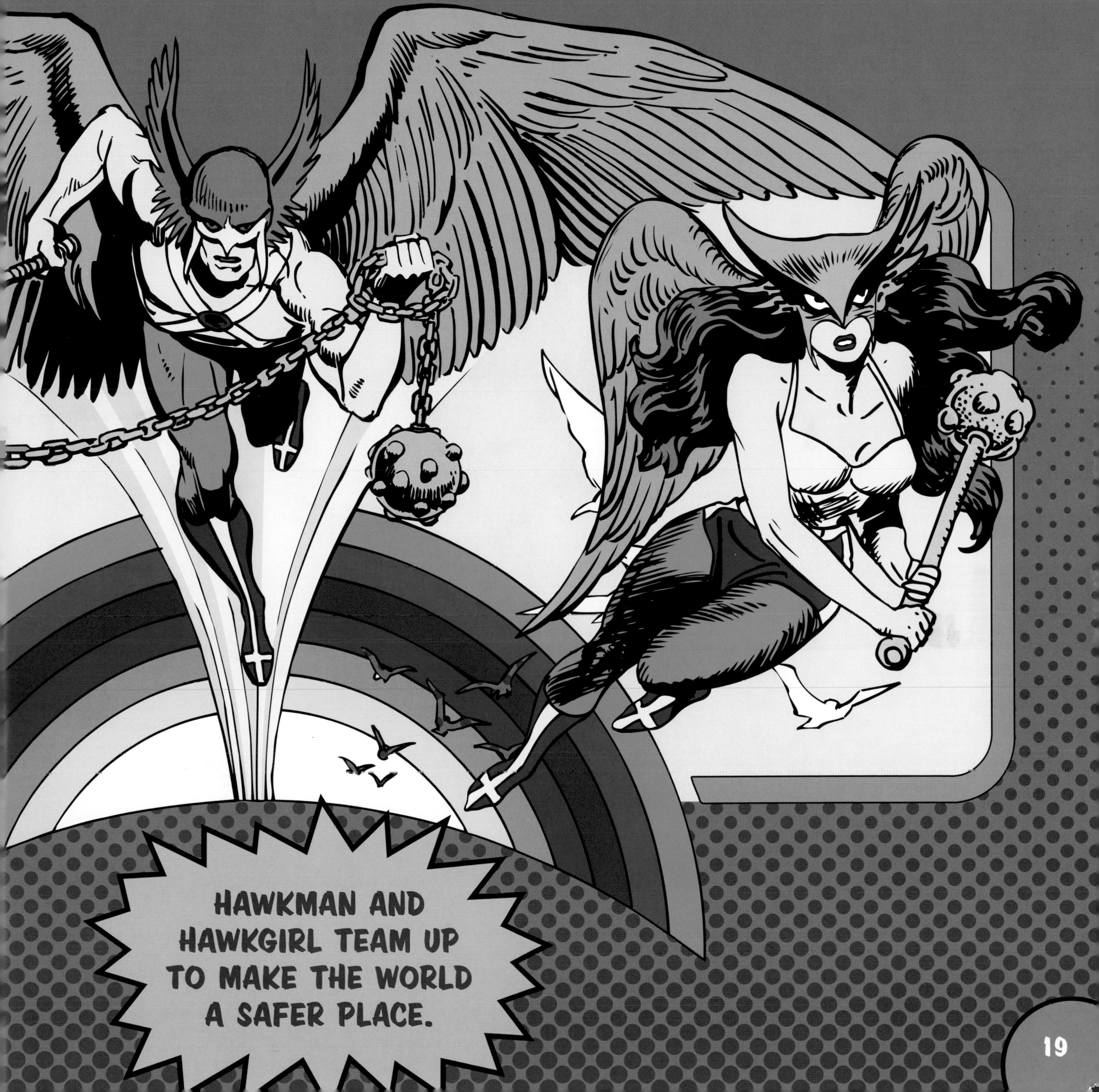
HAWKMAN AND
HAWKGIRL TEAM UP
TO MAKE THE WORLD
A SAFER PLACE.

CYBORG

Cyborg started out as an athletic boy named Victor Stone. When he was a teenager, he was in a terrible accident that nearly killed him. The only way to keep him alive was to replace most of his body with mechanical parts. It turned out these mechanical body parts worked really well—so well that they gave him super-strength, serious brainpower, and a new name, Cyborg.

When he was with his old friends, he was a little bit embarrassed about the way he looked with his mechanical parts. But he made new friends—Robin, Starfire, and Raven—and began working with them as part of a team called Teen Titans.

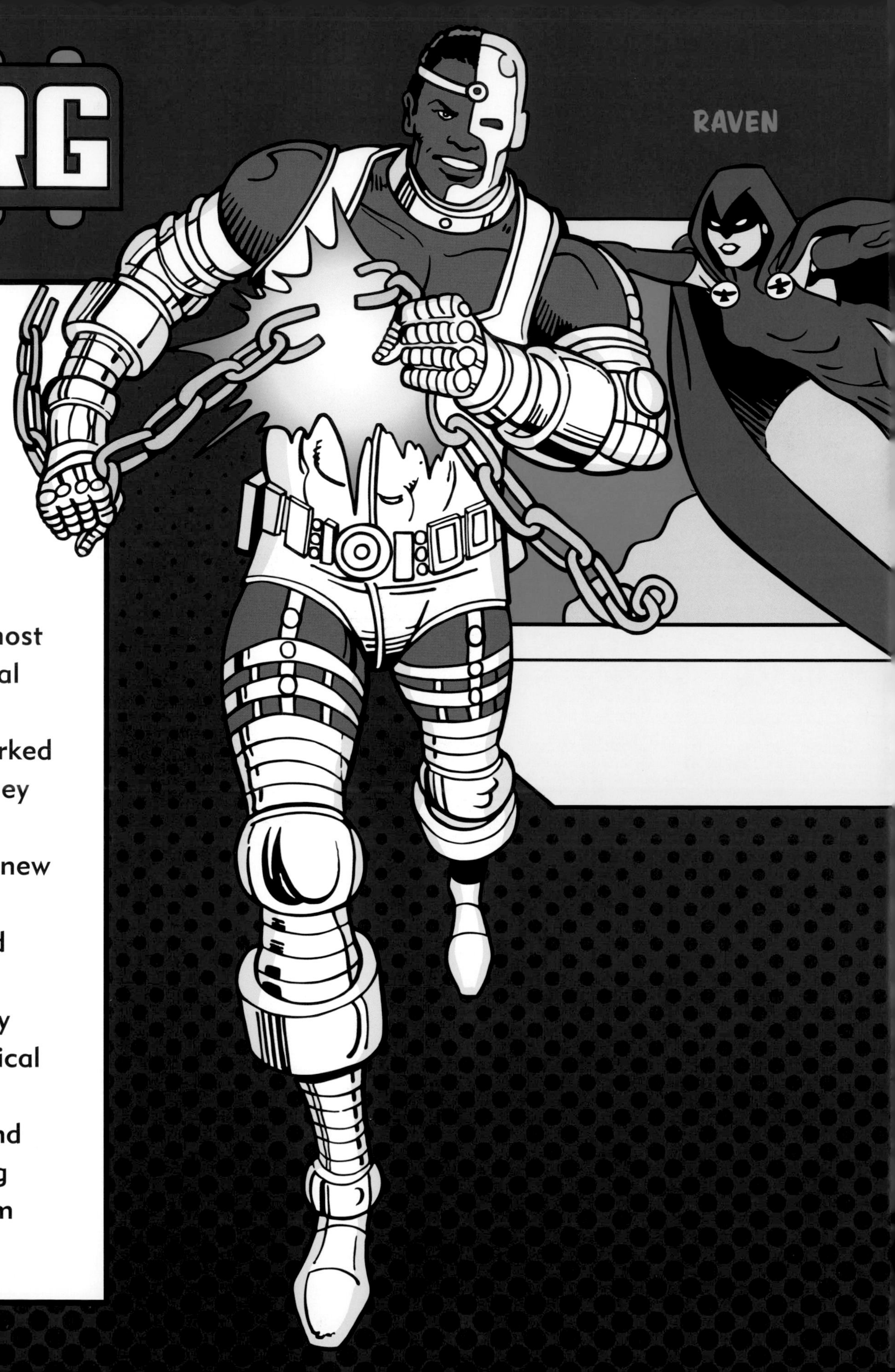
RAVEN

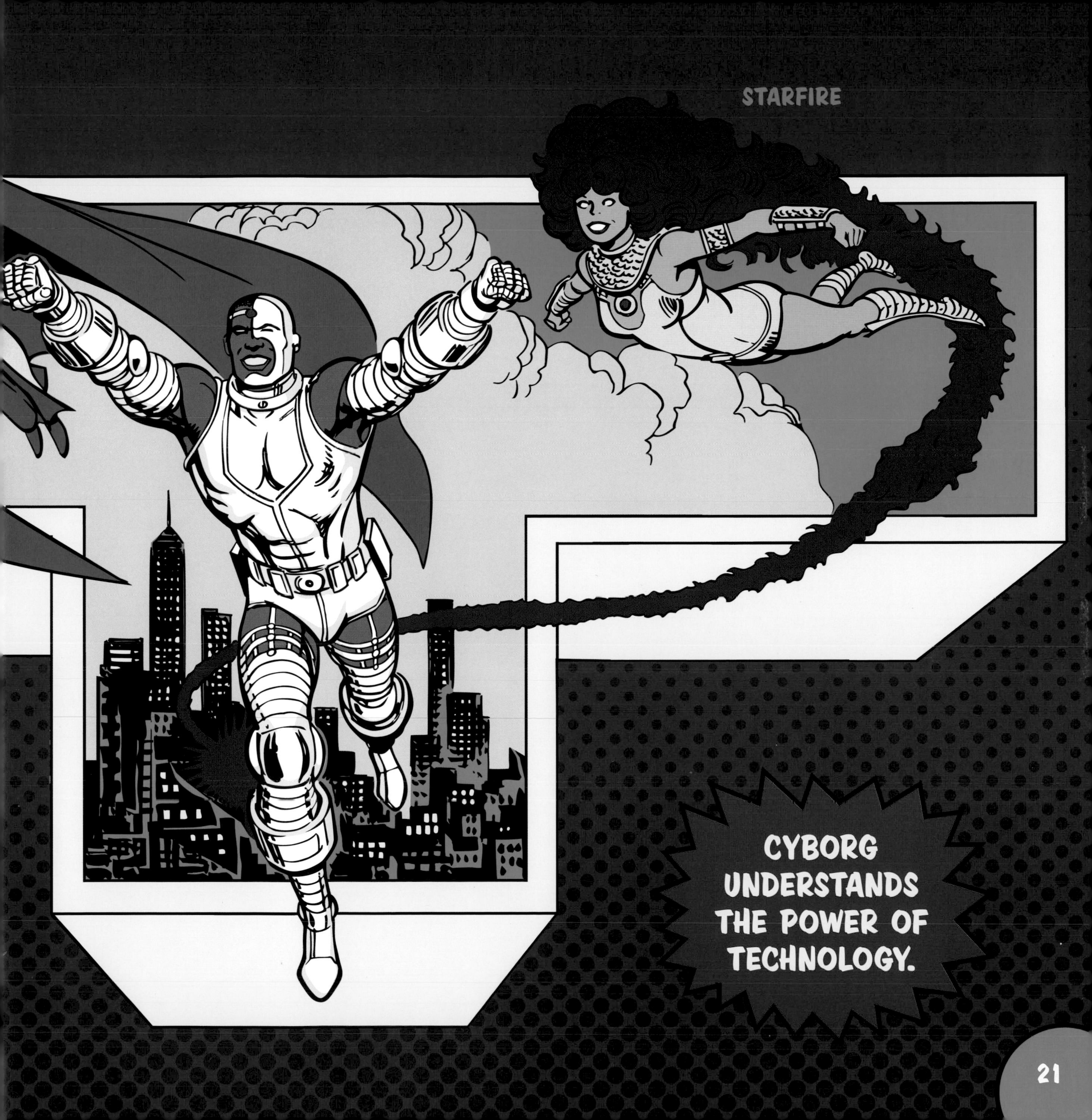
STARFIRE
CYBORG UNDERSTANDS THE POWER OF TECHNOLOGY.

MARTIAN MANHUNTER

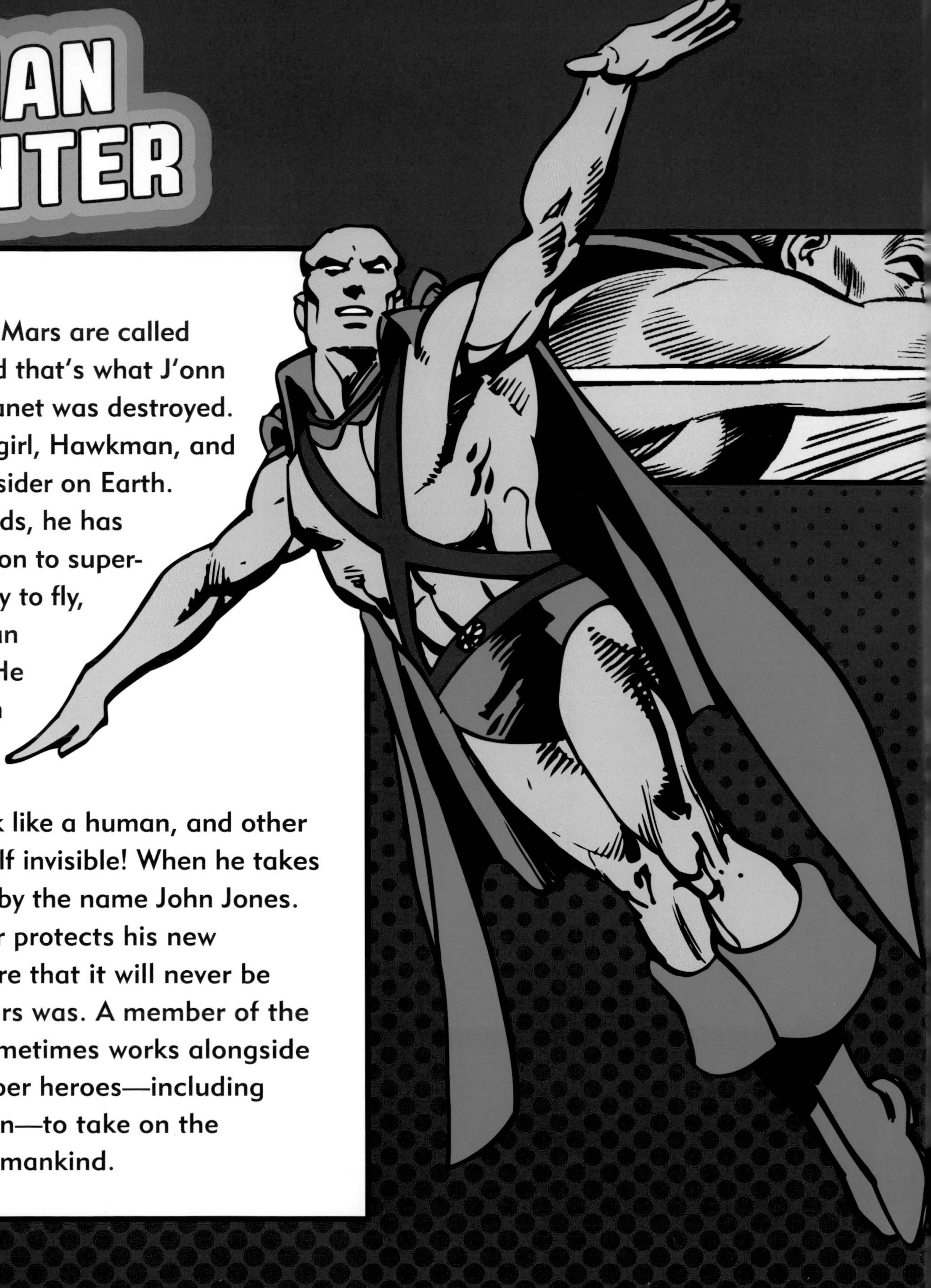

Police officers on Mars are called manhunters, and that's what J'onn J'onzz was until his planet was destroyed. Like Superman, Supergirl, Hawkman, and Hawkgirl, he is an outsider on Earth. And like his alien friends, he has alien powers. In addition to super-strength and the ability to fly, Martian Manhunter can read people's minds. He can even walk through walls and other solid objects! Sometimes he shape-shifts to look like a human, and other times he makes himself invisible! When he takes human form, he goes by the name John Jones.

Martian Manhunter protects his new home, Earth, to be sure that it will never be destroyed the way Mars was. A member of the Justice League, he sometimes works alongside other unstoppable super heroes—including Superman and Batman—to take on the greatest threats to humankind.

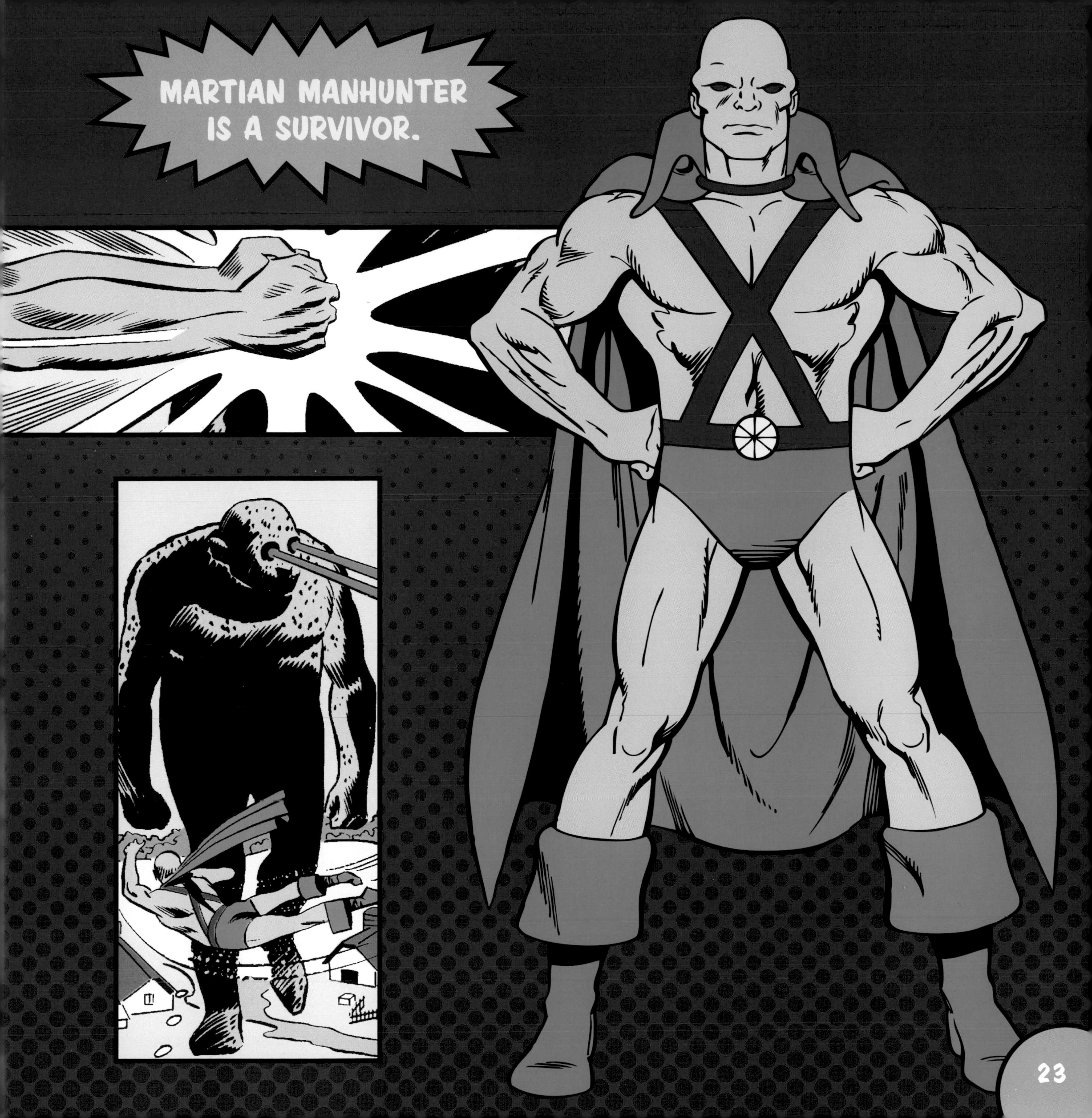
MARTIAN MANHUNTER IS A SURVIVOR.

AQUAMAN

Aquaman is the king of the undersea world of Atlantis. He communicates with sea creatures who help him patrol all seven oceans of the world. He has incredible strength and can swim faster than any fish in the ocean. Aquaman and his wife, Mera, can live and fight on land as well as underwater. Together, they fearlessly take on any threat to the seas.

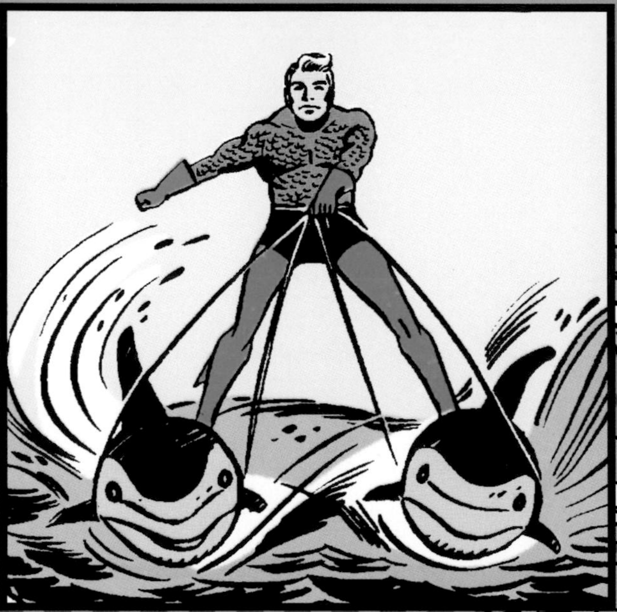

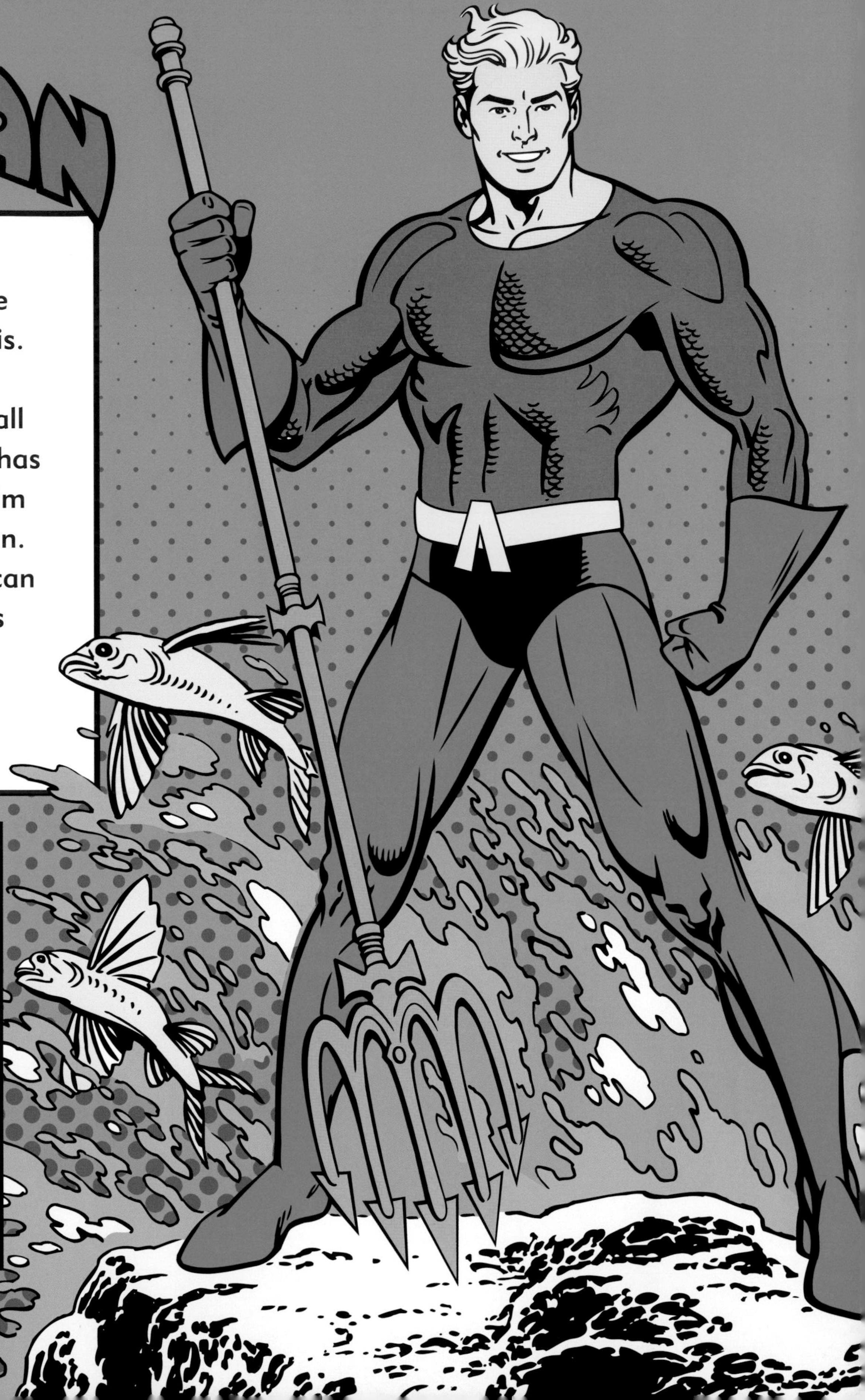

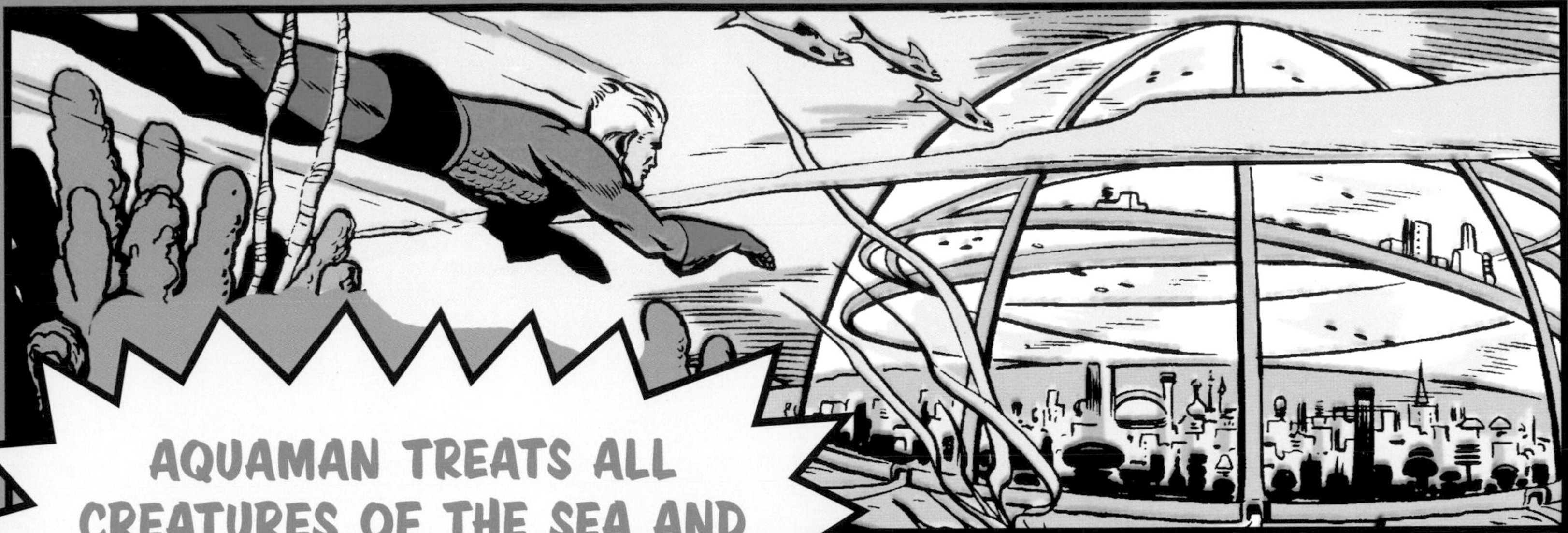

AQUAMAN TREATS ALL CREATURES OF THE SEA AND LAND WITH RESPECT, EARNING THEIR LOYALTY.

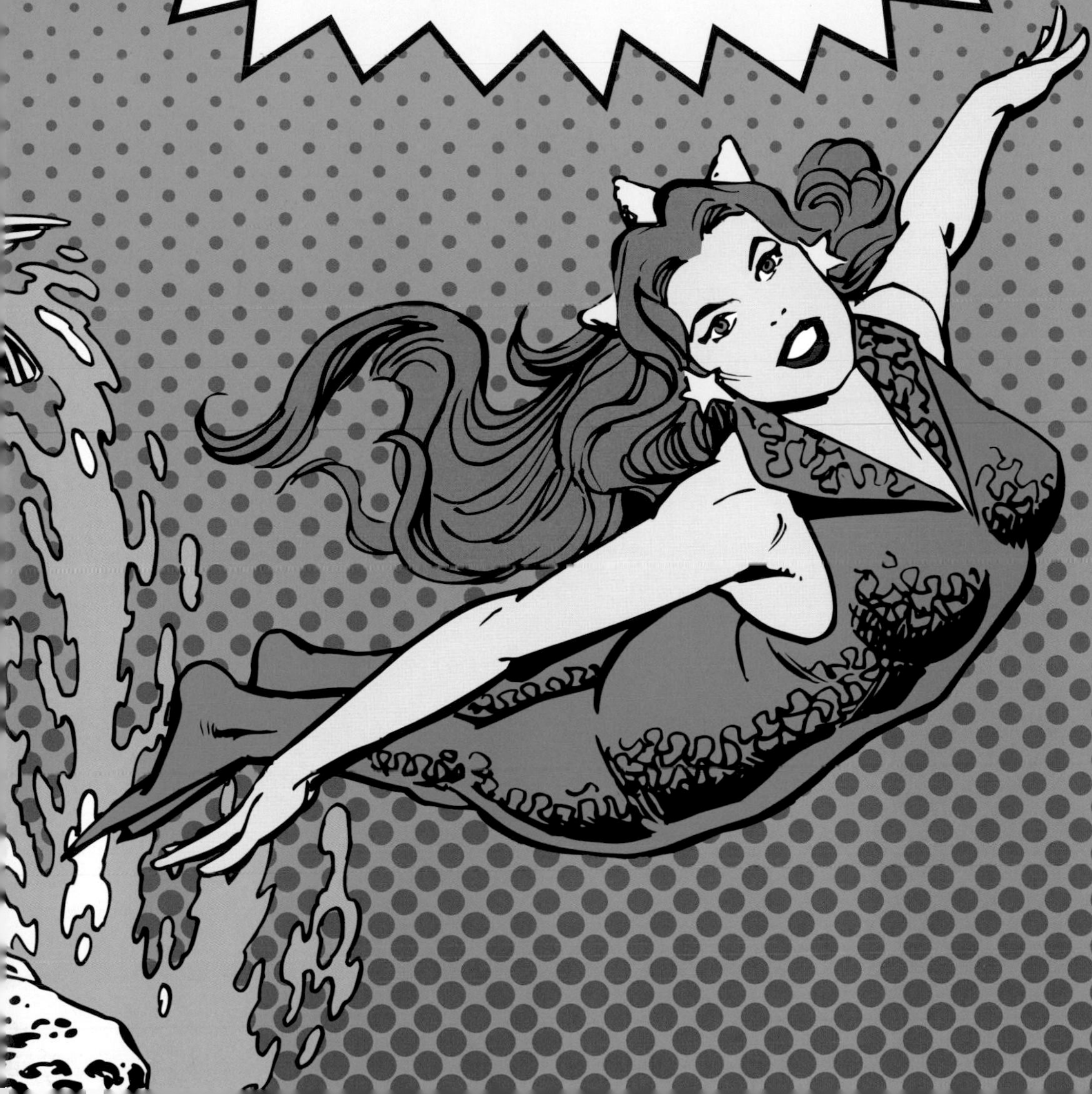

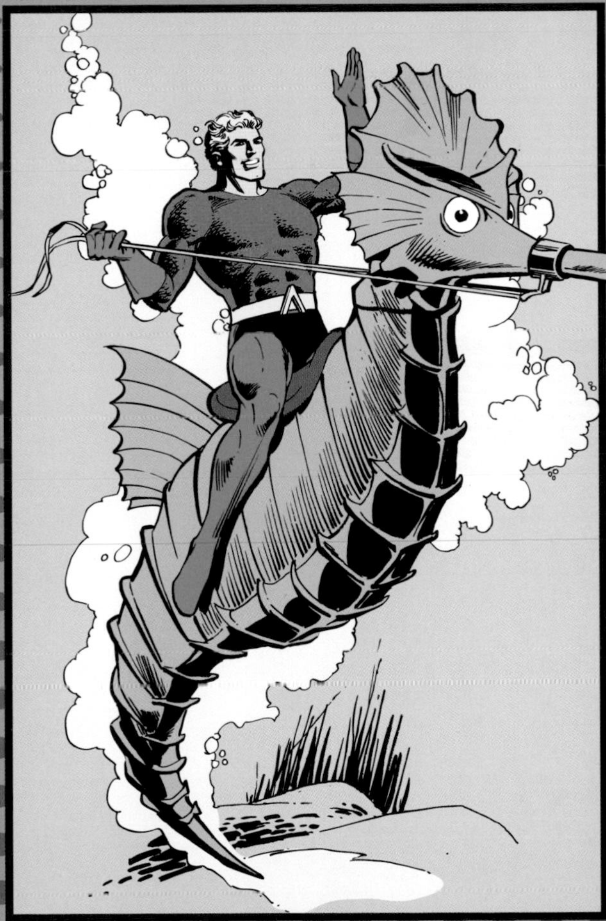

Green Arrow

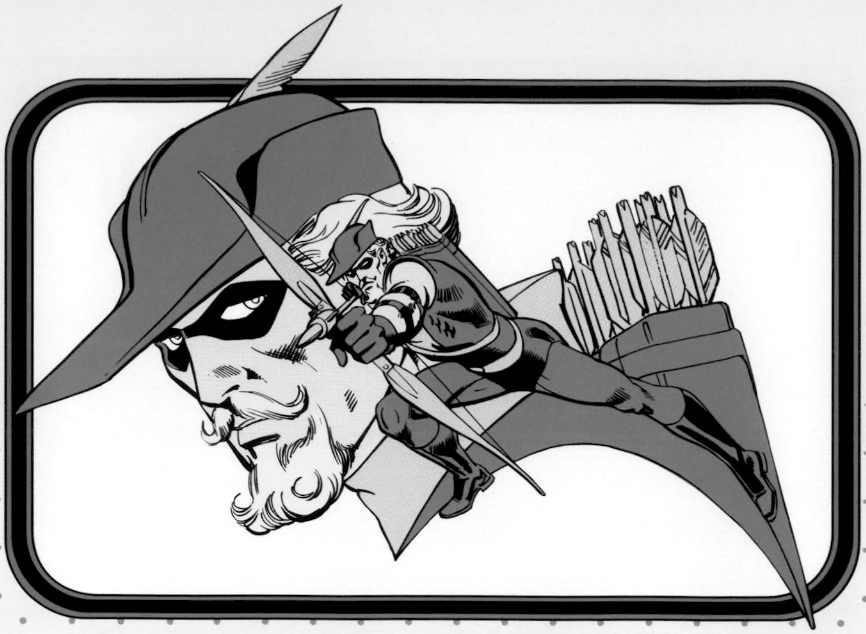

Oliver Queen was a Star City billionaire who did not work very hard or care very much about anyone other than himself. Then he was in a boating accident. The boat sank, and he washed up on an uncharted island. There, he had to learn how to survive on his own. He taught himself how to hunt and fish so that he could eat. That's how he mastered the art of using a bow and arrow. Years later, when he got off of the island, he was a changed man. In addition to working hard, he was determined to do as much good as he could!

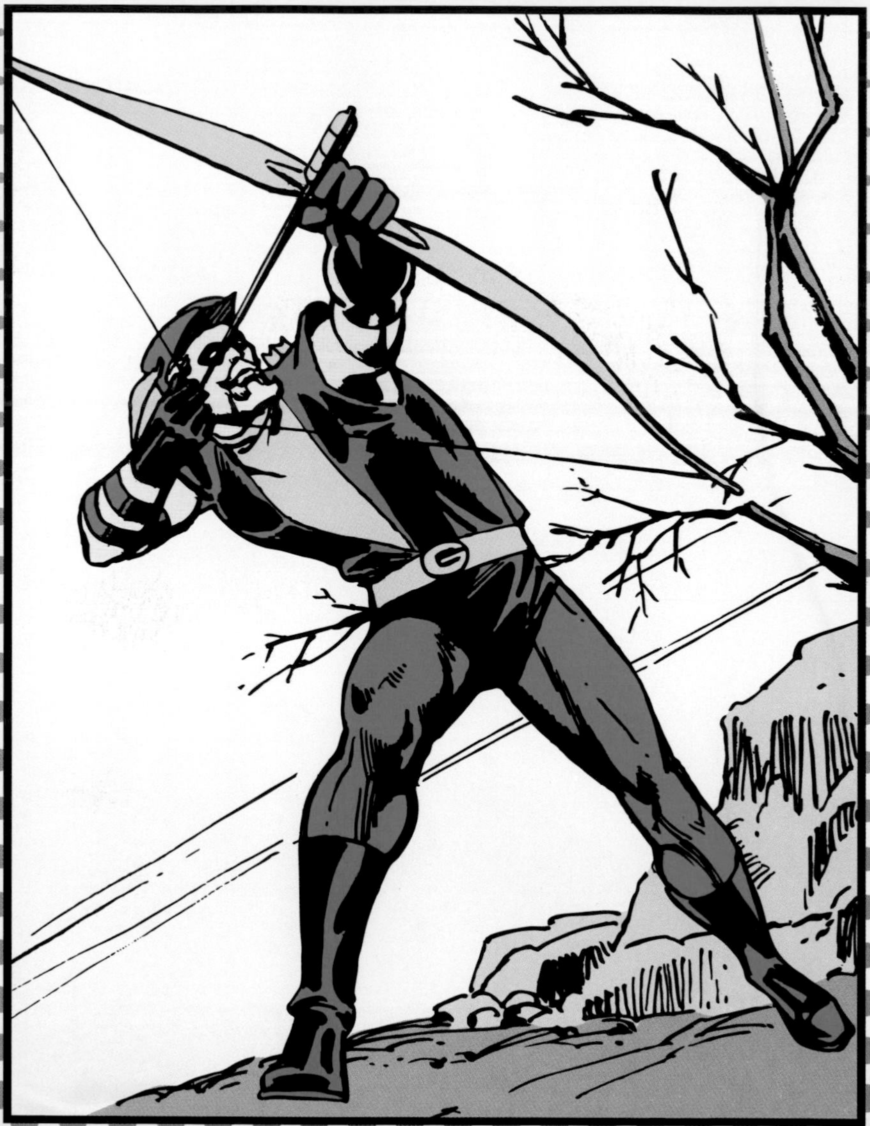

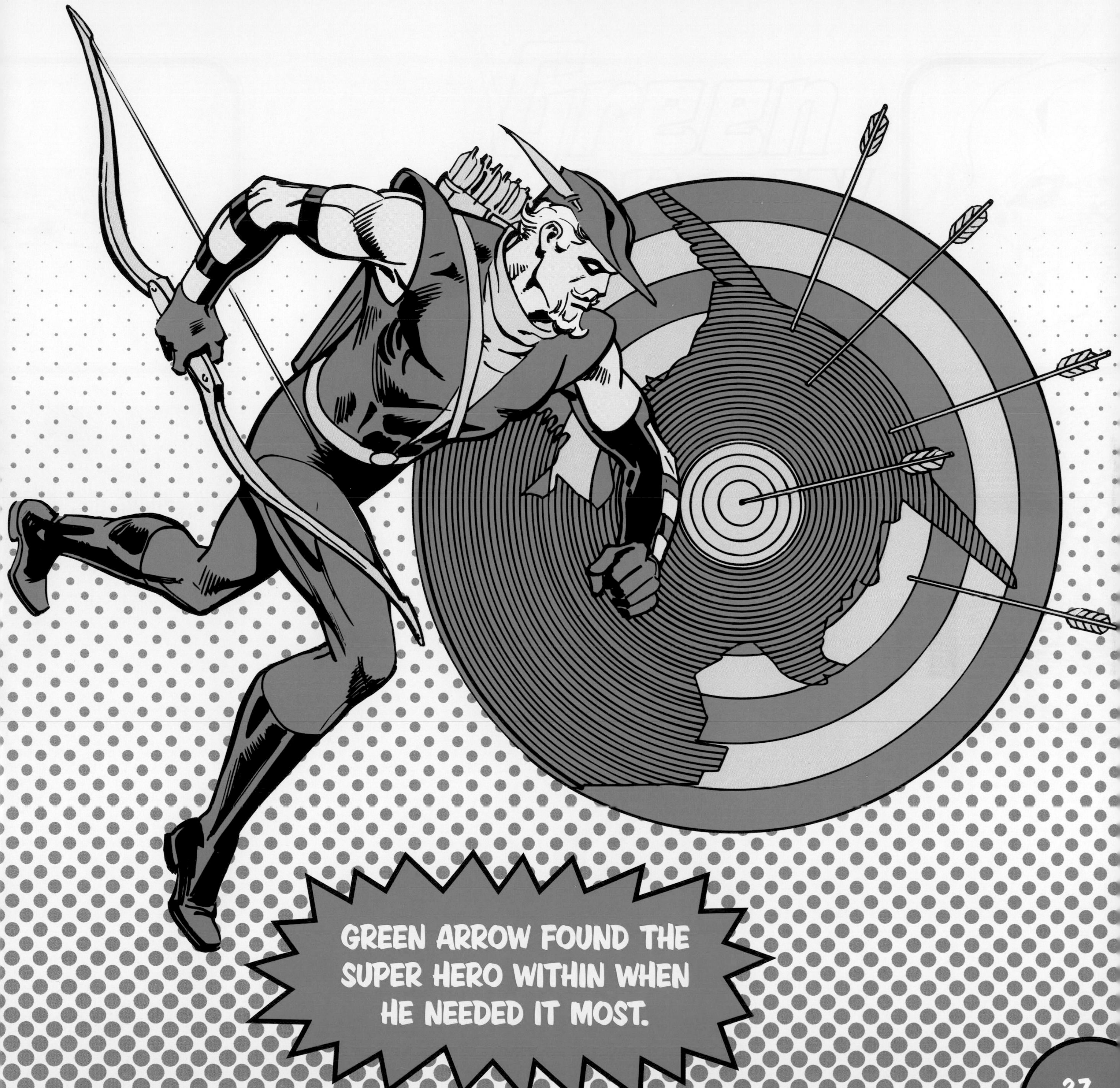
GREEN ARROW FOUND THE
SUPER HERO WITHIN WHEN
HE NEEDED IT MOST.

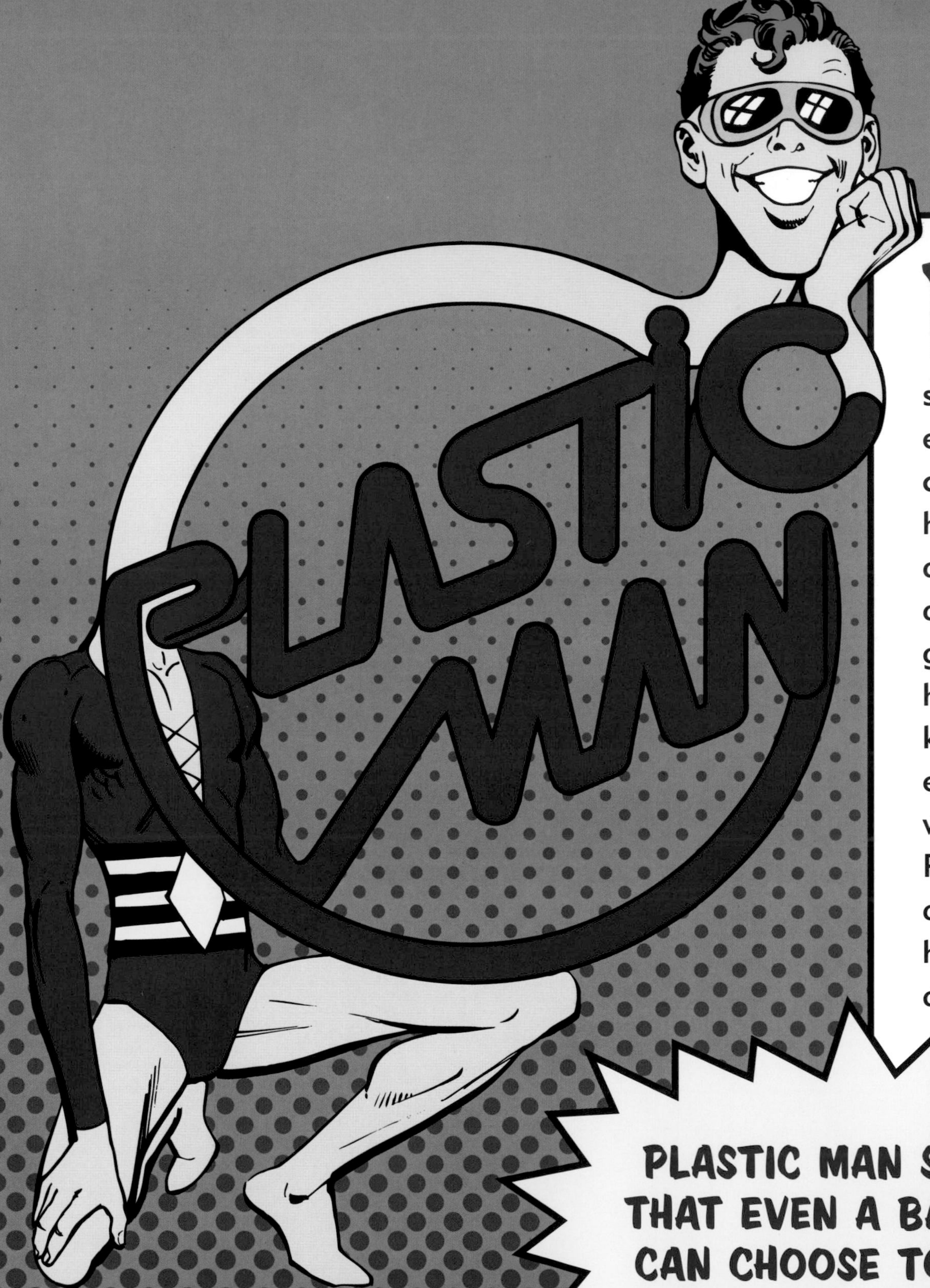
PLASTIC MAN

Patrick "Eel" O'Brian did not start out as a super hero either. He was a petty criminal! One night, he was cracking a safe at a chemical factory, and he was caught by a guard. He was injured in his shoulder, and some kind of liquid chemical entered his body. He woke up . . . elastic! As Plastic Man, he can twist and stretch and contort his body into pretty much any shape.

PLASTIC MAN SHOWS THAT EVEN A BAD GUY CAN CHOOSE TO BE A SUPER HERO INSTEAD.

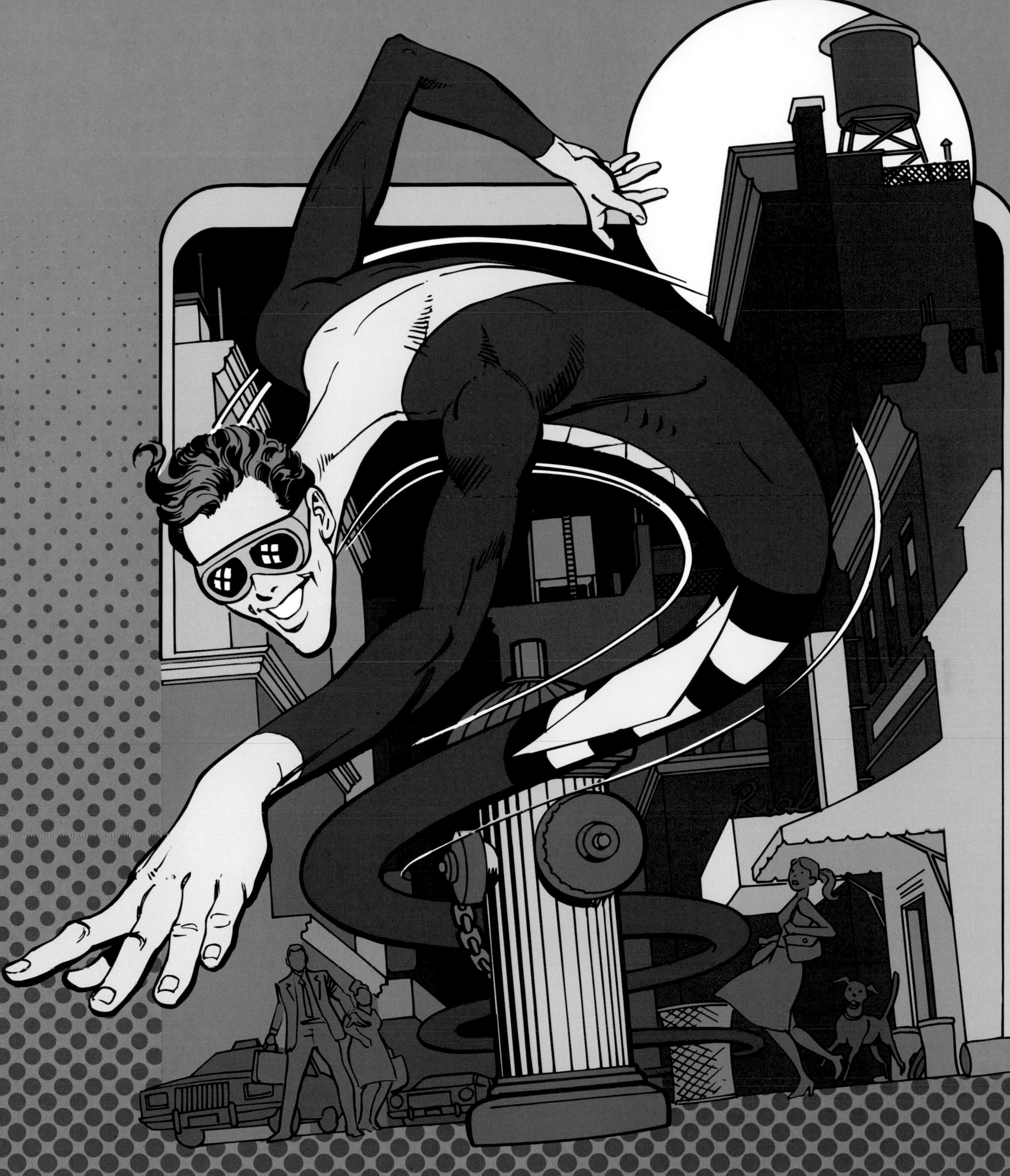

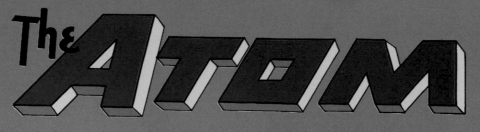

The Atom

Ray Palmer was once a regular-size man—one with an outsize brain. Working as a physicist, he discovered a star whose energy caused objects to shrink. He developed a belt filled with this star matter and tested it on himself. Sure enough, he shrunk!

Although his body became much smaller, he still had the strength of a full-size man! The Atom's ability to make himself teeny means that he can explore places where no one else can go—like inside a wire or into somebody's bloodstream!

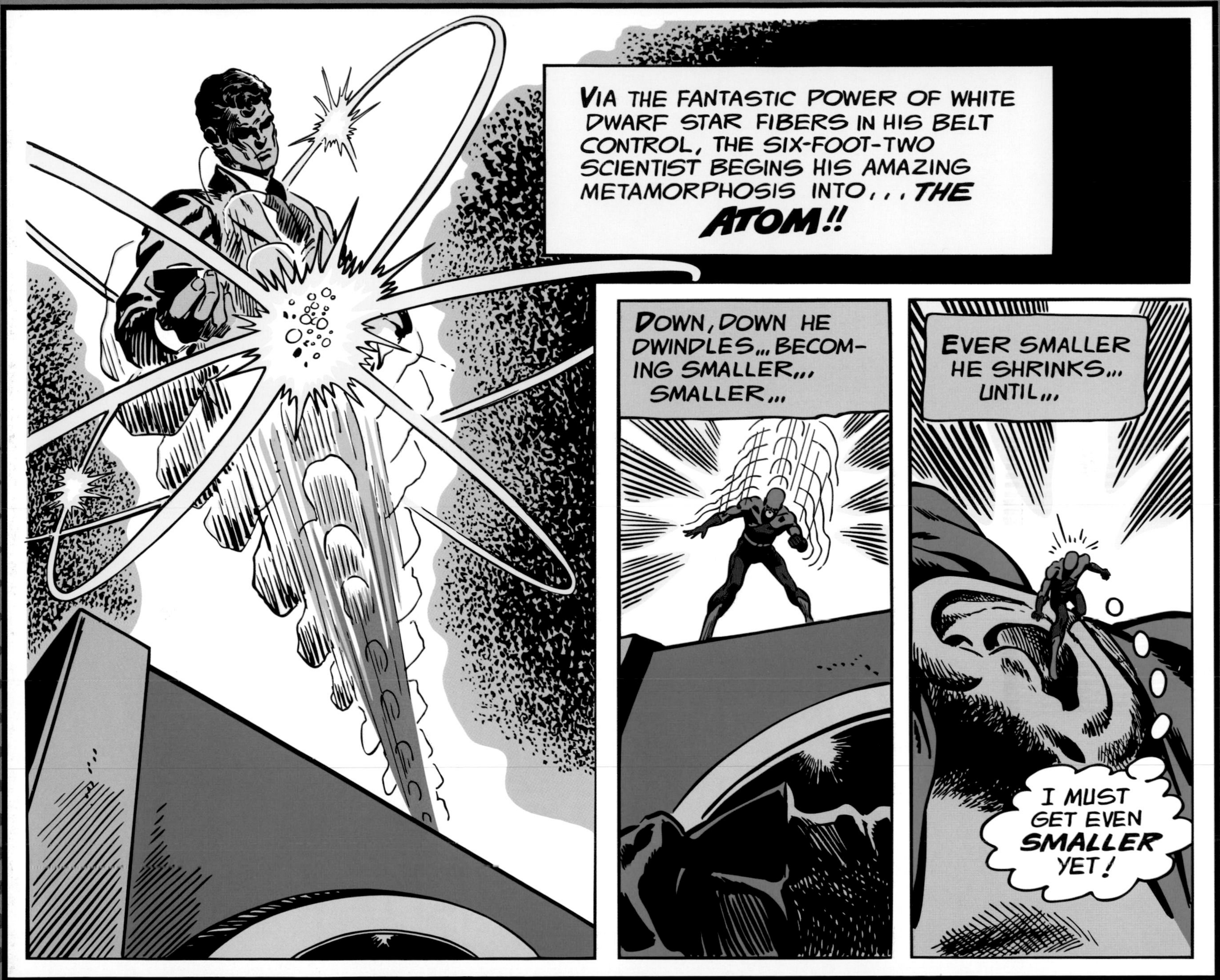
VIA THE FANTASTIC POWER OF WHITE DWARF STAR FIBERS IN HIS BELT CONTROL, THE SIX-FOOT-TWO SCIENTIST BEGINS HIS AMAZING METAMORPHOSIS INTO... THE ATOM!!
DOWN, DOWN HE DWINDLES... BECOMING SMALLER... SMALLER...
EVER SMALLER HE SHRINKS... UNTIL...
I MUST GET EVEN SMALLER YET!

TREMENDOUS POWER CAN COME IN A TINY PACKAGE.

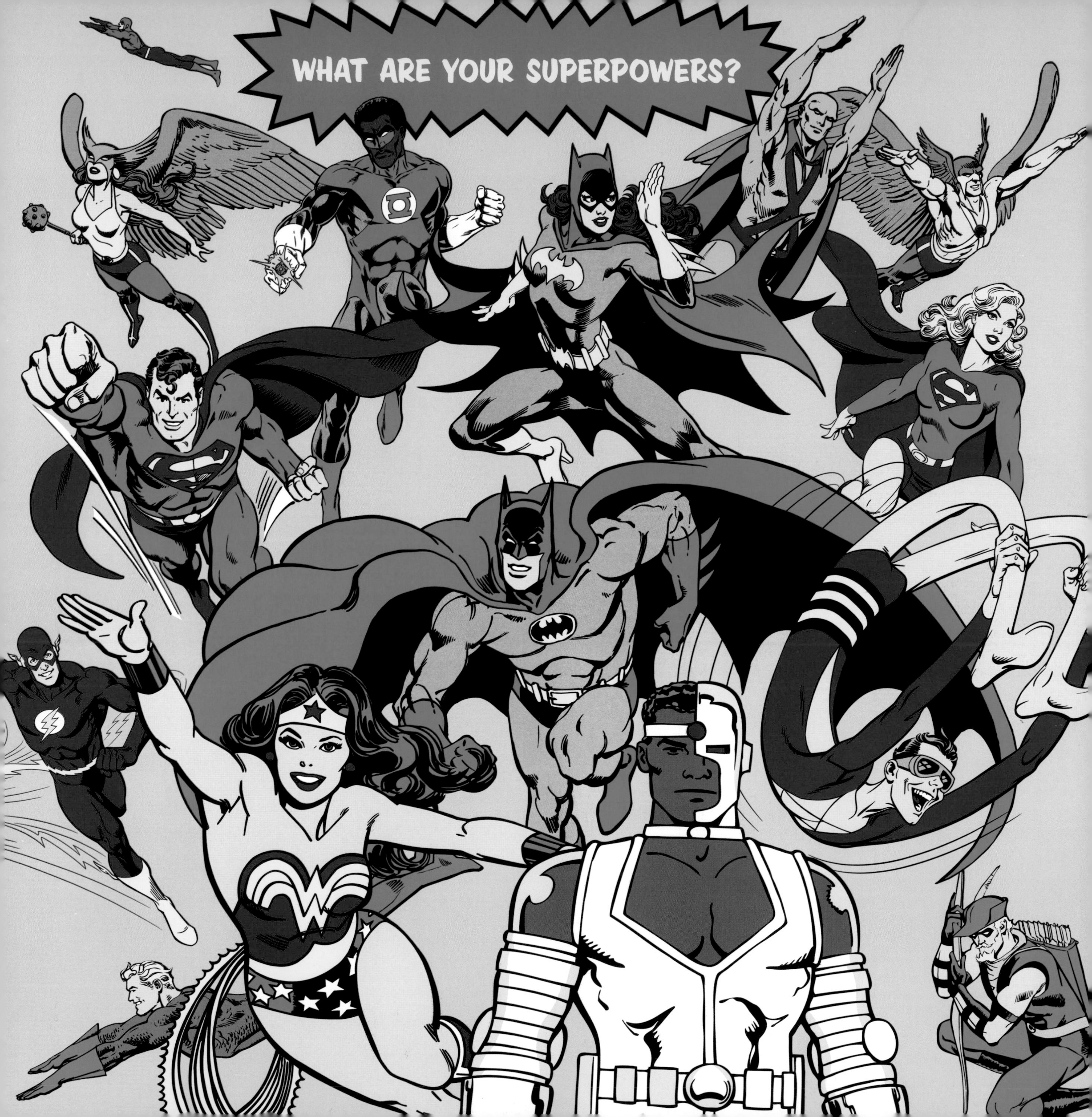
WHAT ARE YOUR SUPERPOWERS?

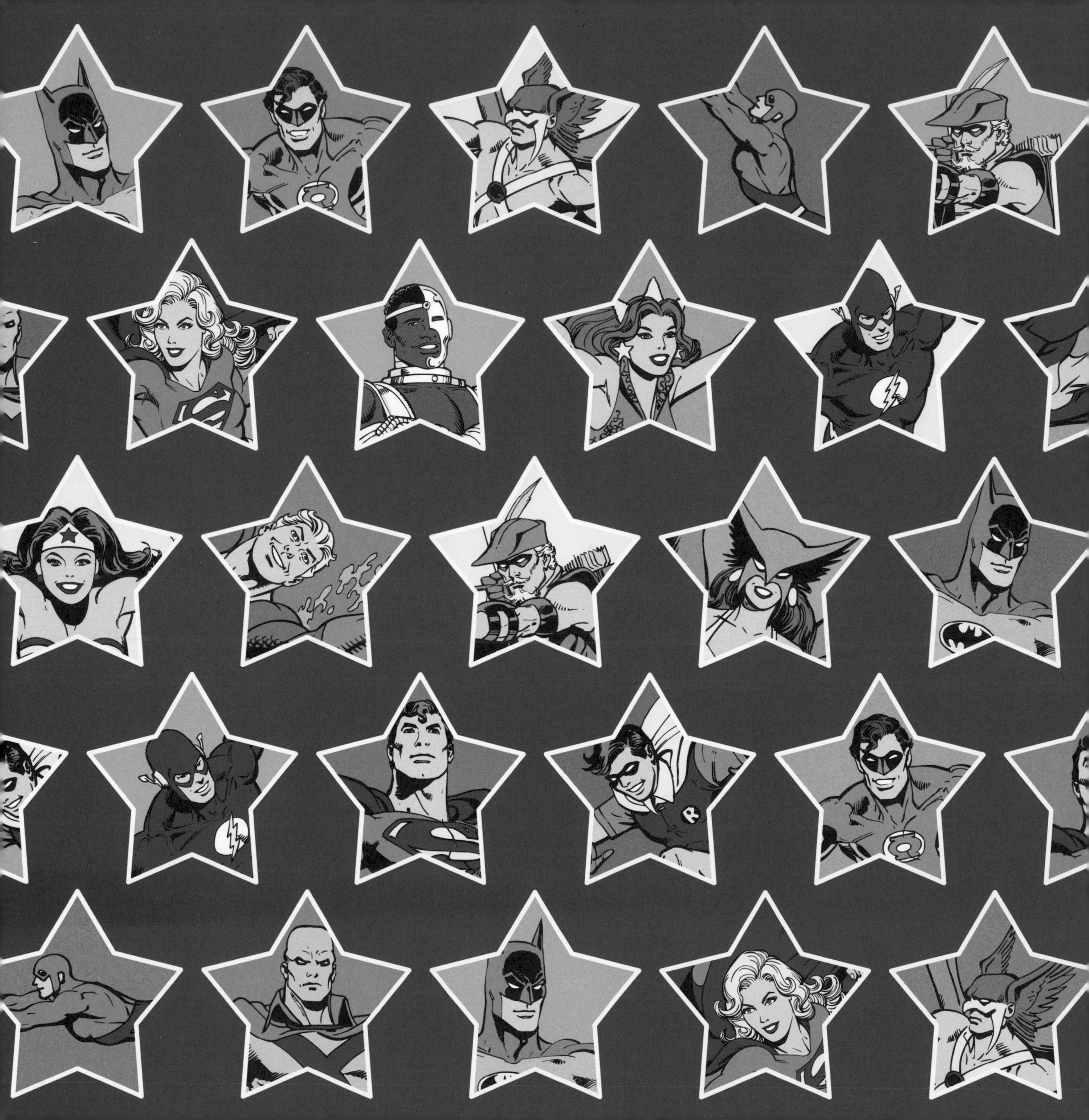